THE AUTHOR

CW00829160

Half English, half Welsh, Nick Cann was
born in South West London in 1959.
Since 1981 he has worked as a magazine,
newspaper and book designer.
In 1989 he moved to Northern Ireland
where he works as a journalist and
editorial design consultant.
Jake's Eulogy is his first published novel.

JAKE'S EULOGY

BY NICK CANN

indiego.co.uk

FIRST PUBLISHED IN THE UK IN 2005 BY

indiego

HOLYWOOD, COUNTY DOWN

© indiego 2005

TEXT © NICK CANN

ALL RIGHTS RESERVED

Nick Cann is hereby identified as author of this work in accordance with
section 77 of the copyright, designs & patents act 1988

ISBN: 0 9549066 0 8

COVER PHOTO: ROMAS FOORD

DESIGN: NICK CANN

PROOF READING: BRIAN CANN, JANE HARRISON & RICHARD KENNEDY

PRINTED BY EASYPRINT, BELFAST

BINDING: ROBINSON & MORNIN, BELFAST

FOR SIMON MORGAN

ACKNOWLEDGMENTS:

Jake's poem on page 186 was inspired by "Tonight I Can Write" (Translated by WS Merwin, from *Selected Poems by Pablo Neruda,* published by Jonathan Cape)

"Life On Mars" Words and Music by David Bowie © 1971 Reproduced by permission of EMI Music Publishing Ltd/ Chrysalis Music Ltd/Moth Music/Tintoretto Music, London

WITH THANKS TO:

Pat, Sophie & Chloe, Brian & Sheila, Wendy & Judy

1.

"For old man's eye, my dears,
For old man's eye,
We'll drink a cup of kindness here,
For the sake of old man's eye..."

Thirty years of singing *Auld Lang Syne* and Jake McCullough still didn't know the words, but it was his party piece, whatever the month or season – it was mid-October. He had been singing it his way for so long that it was too late to change now. It was at least phonetically correct.

Tonight he was slurring the words so badly, however, that he could have been singing the words of *The Fields of Athenry* to the tune of *Anarchy in the UK*. Never mind, he was in good company, for he was not the only late-night crooner clinging to the bar as if it were a theme park ride.

"We'll drink a cup of kindness here,
For the sake of old man's eye..."

The rest of the group, a dozen drunkards, doubled up with laughter at the end of the chorus. Singing through persistent fits of the giggles was becoming a challenge. If it weren't for the enthusiasm of the four burly Texans, they would have collapsed in a heap long ago.

Another song over and Jake McCullough slumped forward until his head rested on the bar. He knew the inability to hold it upright signalled the necessity to retreat to his bed. Sliding off the bar stool and staggering out of the room, he resisted the opportunity to join in *Swing Low Sweet Chariot,* which was being sung in honour of the Texans, members of the Houston Seventh Day Tabernacle Gospel Choir, for the fourth or fifth time.

As he left, Jake McCullough forgot to pick up the Sputnik-like trophy he had received a couple of hours earlier. It now sat jettisoned on the counter beside a half-drunk pint.

Millions had been lavished on the Royal Pavilion Hotel, Brighton, to transform it into a venue fit for conferences and social events. On the Friday night Jake McCullough was in residence, the revolving doors had whisked in an exotic mix of penguin-suited men and scantily clad women attending one of many awards shows to be held in the Regency ballroom now that year end was nigh. Tonight's event: a literary awards dinner.

If the *Northern and West Building Society Literary Awards* were not supported by the highbrow, few of the mainstream writers cared. The evening was a fun night out, a release for members of a profession who were, by and large, self-employed and spent most of their time working in isolation. The event presented an opportunity to enjoy the company of peers and sniff around the scattering of agents and publishers when they could be caught with a drink in hand.

The post-dinner celebrations were raucous and, for the hard core of early hour revellers, unruly. Neither social status nor education, intelligence, income nor wit could offer much resistance to the temptations of the free bar.

By two o'clock in the morning Jake McCullough had drunk enough booze to keep a small chain of off-licences in stock for a month. His achievement in winning the award for *'Best New Writer in Children's Publishing'* had come as a genuine surprise to him. Initially he was ecstatic, having barely been aware of his nomination.

Since he had recently turned thirty-five he thought it ironic that he could still be considered a new writer. Even though he knew that any success should be tasted and found sweet, he couldn't help feeling disappointed that his serious work – the three-hundred-page novels, of which only two out of the five had been published – was yet to be recognised. Never a good review. Never a nomination. Never an award.

It was his children's book character, Johnny-One-Foot, the Footballing Penguin that had been his success. *Johnny-One-Foot*, first penned in biro on a napkin for his children's entertainment, had become a national icon earning him a comfortable living from TV rights and merchandising. Johnny's popularity had only exacerbated Jake's lack of fulfilment.

In the short term, however, he enjoyed the company of his new friends and drank long and hard to their, his, and anybody-else-who-came-into-their-orbit's good health. And now he had taken his fill of sycophancy, and with *Swing Low Sweet Chariot* still echoing from the bar, managed to fumble his way to his landing on the first floor, find his door, find his key, stab it into the lock and pour himself through the doorway into the claustrophobic environment of his hotel room – soundproof and suffocating.

The bed beckoned. Lured by the promise of greater comfort, Jake staggered over and let himself flop backwards like a rag doll onto the ocean of bedspread and pillows. The door swung closed behind him with a snug thud, shutting out the drunken bellowing of the American gospel choir and plunging the room into silence, sealing the world out from his solitary confinement. Sensory deprivation in semi-comfort. After a few moments he let out a sigh that like a punctured tyre expelled stale air in a long and steady breath.

He opened his eyes to stare up at the ceiling and waited for it to start spinning, not wanting to close them again if it did. He didn't want to fall asleep, not yet anyway. He wanted to think a little first. He wanted to understand why, now that the initial euphoria of his triumph had worn off, there was no sense of achievement, no self-satisfaction. Why did he feel such a sense of failure? Why did everything bore him so?

He sat up and nestled his head in his hands, rubbing his face to try and dislodge the alcoholic fug enveloping it, and looked around the room for a distraction. There was little to interest him until his eyes focused on the minibar. Drink? Yes, he needed more. He would escape into a hangover and sit the game out for a while.

The contents of the minibar didn't amount to much – a half bottle of Veuve Clicquot, three bottles of Pilsner lager, three bottles of Bud, Diet Coke, orange juice, some Belgian chocolates, three bags of crisps, a half bottle of gin, a half bottle of vodka, two half bottles of white wine, a half bottle of red, and some miniature bottles of brandy, whisky and cognac.

Drunk, he tottered to and fro as best he could to unburden the minibar of its booty, placing the bottles neatly on the dressing table by the window, meticulously arranging them in a uniform row. It took a huge physical effort to be delicate, and mammoth powers of concentration not to knock the bottles over like skittles. His hands were more reliable than his legs. His hands trembled, but could be controlled. His legs were steady enough until he tried to walk, when movement in a straight line seemed beyond them. The image of a newborn foal came to mind.

The booze on the dressing table multiplied quickly; the overall bottlescape enhanced by the broad mirror at the back which doubled its mass. As he loaded the bottles onto the table Jake was startled by what at first he took for an apparition of his father – a greyer face with greying blue eyes. For a moment or two he searched the reflection for the face of his youth, surveying the new contours, checking the development of the double chin, inspecting his nose and ears for shoots of old man's hair, and stroking his floppy quiff back into place.

His hair. At least he had his hair. And his teeth were fine. He gave himself a toothy grin and inspected his realigned smile. But God, they were white. Somehow, and considering the abuse he had inflicted upon himself over the years, he didn't look *too* bad. In fact he looked pretty good. People always said he looked five years younger. He wasn't unattractive. He could tell by the way women still glanced at him on the street from time to time and the attention he attracted at parties, but he knew he couldn't keep it up for much longer. Sooner rather than later his looks would go down the drain, wasted like the slops of a drunken binge, once fine wine.

Driven by a renewed thirst, he fetched a clean glass from the complimentary tea and coffee tray and took it into the bathroom for rinsing. He wandered back into the bedroom to switch on the radio, buffing the glass on a fresh facecloth.

A smile illuminated his dour expression as the familiar sound of Radio Four's *Just a Minute* filled the room. A late-night repeat from far away on long wave, where Nicholas Parsons presided over a group of celebrities attempting to talk on a given subject for sixty seconds without pause. The current subject was '*Why I like cheese-and-wine parties*'.

The chatter on the radio, he thanked God, drowned out the faint drunken hubbub from the ballroom, the rain lashing the window and, from a distant floor, the steady rhythm of a bed thumping against a wall.

Now Jake was ready to commence his party for one. Reclining in the armchair between the bed and the stash of bottles, he steadied himself for the 'off', cursing that he had no lemon or ice for the spirits.

The idea hatched in his mind that he would try to drink the minibar dry. YES. He'd drink the bloody lot. He would start at the top and work down. That is to say, he would drink the Veuve Clicquot, then the wine, then the beer. He would drink the spirits last – drinking vodka, then gin, then whisky, then brandy, then cognac, in that order.

His expectation was that he wouldn't get round to drinking the spirits, hoping that the champagne, wine and beer, on top of the huge quantity of free booze, especially the cocktails he had had earlier, would be enough to render him unconscious first.

The Veuve Clicquot popped, he grabbed a bag of crisps and settled down to begin his feast. At first the champagne tasted refreshing, but two glasses down – large glasses – it became less palatable. The effervescence on top of his earlier consumption was beginning to make him feel bloated. He also felt weary. His eyes were sore, the lids heavy, and he could sense that they were blinking more regularly and that the strokes were getting slower and longer. Though he tried to fight it, his head rolled forward and he was sleeping before a third glass could be poured.

The next day came too soon. Mid-morning he was woken by the ringing of the telephone, then found the damp patch in his trousers where he had spilled his last drink. People were looking for him – his agent, his wife, his children. His head was splitting. As ever, his hangover came accompanied by a scintilla of guilt.

Jake peeled off his dinner suit, a worn and battered skin not quite ready to go, and crawled back into bed for two or three hours, letting the day into his life in small degrees, just as much as his hangover would allow. He would wake up, then sit up, and if his head was sore lie down again and go back to sleep for another half an hour.

After four or five attempts he felt well enough to prise himself out of bed and order a breakfast. It was two o'clock in the afternoon, but might have been dawn or dusk as far as he was aware.

Jake gathered his wits in between nibbles on dried toast. What to do next? Should he get his act together and go home to the security of his wife and children and resume the struggle of his writing career, or should he go haywire and disappear on a two- or three-day bender? Anything would be better than having to face the tedious life he had grown to despise back in North London, the humdrum everyday greyness that he had allowed to become his routine. The tide of his ambition had swept him so far out to sea, that there was no turning back now, no lifebelt. He felt he must drown.

In a flash, a deliciously dark and sinister idea sparked his imagination, as he thought of a much easier way out of the predicament. It involved an exciting new challenge. A kind of nightmarish game. The idea brought him some comfort. If he were to attempt it, and succeed, the act would relieve him of his ongoing headache and solve his problems at a stroke. And if it didn't work, if he failed, the attempt would at least make others sit up and appreciate him more than they had of late.

The idea was simple. He would drink himself to death. Why not? He had tried most things, so why not suicide? He had been drinking himself to death for the past twenty years or so anyway. Now he would speed up the process. He loved drink and drinking, and in the same way that some people fancy laughing to death, or dying mid-orgasm, believed that this would be his preferred option given a choice, a painless one at that – less painful than the sclerosis he was sipping his way towards. It would be quick and enjoyable. And he was a writer; suicide might even be the making of him. Yes, it would be a career move. Others had tried it with some success.

Jake addressed the logistics whilst finishing his breakfast. If he were going to get drunk – drunk enough to kill himself – it would take more than the remaining contents of the minibar to do it. The booze would have to be delivered by van from a wine merchant. This was practical; he would require volume, after all. It would have to be vodka, because it was clean and he would be able to drink it in large quantities mixed with a little orange juice. Just enough to give it a pleasant taste. A few bottles of gin and vermouth would be required to mix up the occasional dry martini to break the monotony of the diet of vodka and orange. He might even get a few six packs of Budweiser to quench his thirst first thing in the morning – if he had mornings.

Whether he could drink himself to death in just three days he didn't know, but was sure that if he drank fast enough, it was possible that he could poison himself on the first night alone. He guessed that he probably hadn't been far off achieving that on the previous night. Firstly however, he would have to notify the hotel that he would be staying on for an extra couple of days and having some books delivered – three or four boxes. Yes, that would satisfy their curiosity.

The alternative to 'Plan A' was less attractive. It required mental stamina and concentration, and meant embracing normality. He didn't think that he had too much stock of either stamina or concentration left in him. To go home now, feeling as demoralised as he did, and continue barking up the wrong tree wasn't what he wanted any more. He had exhausted too many last chances.

He considered his kids and what was best for them, but couldn't continue the train of thought. It was just too painful to contemplate how he would be letting them down and too great an obstacle to achieving the present objective. When he thought about his wife he felt sick. What this would do to her confirmed his lowest opinion of himself, but he suspected that she would cope, could rebuild her life.

No, he couldn't go on hurting people. Far better to go out with a bang. He got up, got out the Yellow Pages and looked up *Wine and Spirit Merchants…Wholesale.*

When Jake's contraband arrived in the foyer he had trouble getting it delivered to his room. The duty manager grew suspicious of the contents – books that clinked. A severe test of Jake's diplomatic skills.

For once Jake was unable to offer a hand to the delivery man. He often liked to help out. It was his way of proving to himself that he wasn't a bourgeois bastard just because he had a bit of brass. He didn't like to appear flash, preferring to be 'mates' with everybody. This included delivery people, who were often too busy to pass the time of day with those to whom they were delivering. Jake wasn't convinced that this bonhomie was genuine. He knew that it was inspired by vanity. However, he believed that if he could make a stranger smile and coax a little affection from *them*, then he could reassure himself that for all his other failings, he at least had the common touch. Consequently, few were spared Jake's charm offensive.

The delivery man made two runs to and from his van and was done. Twelve litre bottles of vodka, six bottles of gin, six bottles of vermouth, twelve litres of freshly squeezed orange juice, two bottles of orange squash (just in case he got through the fresh stuff prematurely), forty-eight bottles of Budweiser and thirty-six party-size bags of salt 'n' vinegar crisps.

Jake surveyed his booty, which sat proud on the hotel room floor. Contemplating the booze, a ridiculous amount for one, made him feel nauseous. It also made him laugh.

Being a meticulous type, he had already run a bath in order to keep his hoard as cool as possible. He proceeded to stash a selection of everything in the cold water, a good proportion of which was the beer and orange juice. It would have suited him to store the vodka in a freezer. If he were going to drink vodka, then he would prefer iced vodka from frosted glasses, but never mind. The rest of the booze he arranged neatly in the floorspace of the built-in wardrobe until it was full. The few bottles that were left – mostly beer – he stood in one of the units under the television.

Jake inspected his work with satisfaction, made sure the *Do Not Disturb* notice was in place, found a clean glass, polished it with one of the bathroom towels, breathed on it, buffed it and was ready. A dry martini was mixed using the bathroom as kitchen and bar. He was annoyed that he had forgotten to ask for olives. He withdrew into the bedroom with his drink.

"And your past life a ruined church, let your poison be your cure..."
A toast seemed appropriate.

Sloshing his drink, he turned on the Channel Four racing and sank into the large armchair to watch the 4.15 from Aintree.

By the time it was dark outside, Jake was still waiting to feel drunk, but he persevered. Eventually, he dropped off into a deep sleep. A dry martini and one and a half bottles of vodka down and day one was through.

Jake didn't wake up until lunchtime the next day. This was unfortunate, he thought. If he were going to drink himself to death, he would need to get a move on, or he was going to run out of time. His room was only booked for another day and taking his bank balance into consideration he didn't think he could avoid packing up and going home thereafter.

He would need to stay awake for longer and increase his intake during those hours remaining to him. Not that he wasn't feeling the effect of the previous nights' drinking. He did have the mother of all hangovers and if he weren't so determined to achieve his objective, he would have taken a long sleep to recover.

Revived by a brunch of beer and crisps, he tore into another bottle of vodka. The vodka was starting to work on him, and although he felt *compos mentis*, noticed that he was shakier on his feet and giddy. Whenever he tired of the vodka and orange, he would make himself a dry martini, and each time he mixed one up it was less daintily concocted than the one before. Whereas he had been measuring the ingredients carefully into the stainless steel teapot, which he had commandeered into service as a cocktail shaker, and drinking the cocktail from a freshly washed-up glass, he was now pitching the ingredients into the furry pint mug he had found under the bed, and glugging the rough mixture like beer.

The cocktails were to be his undoing.

On this, the second day of his project, he had given up on the television and had taken to listening to the radio again – Radio Two and Four.

He would much rather have listened to Radio Four to the exclusion of all other stations, but felt that Radio Four's coverage of current affairs would make his mood even more morose than it had been before tuning in. Even drunk into a semi-coma, Jake could sense a pervading atmosphere of gloom on Radio Four, characterised by poorly acted radio plays, angry listeners' letters, cynical interviews and what he considered to be a preference for bad news over good. Since he didn't believe Radio Four to be conducive to good humour, he rationed himself to the odd session of no more than half an hour, punctuated by interludes of the lighter entertainment offered on Radio Two.

By early afternoon he was feeling sleepy again, and couldn't resist the urge to lie down for a brief snooze. Memories of his childhood flooded back – of family holidays in Donegal, the beauty of Kinnagoe Bay and the deserted beach at the far end beyond the rocks with its stream and waterfall. God, how he would love to go back. He pictured his father yelling like a maniac and charging towards the icy sea – the scene unrolling in a gawdy Technicolor of turquoise blues and pillar-box reds – his father turning to smile, a warm and loving smile, reassuring and godly. Then he disappeared, diving into the tall surf.

And as the lullaby strains of the *Desert Island Discs* theme tune drifted across the bedroom ether, he couldn't stop himself from slipping into a deep, deep sleep from which he couldn't awake.

2.

It was obvious that the guest in room 210 was seriously ill. His body language, or lack of it, spoke volumes. When the assistant manager and one of the porters plucked up the courage to open the door with their passkey, they were immediately disturbed by the stifling odour of stale alcohol and the sea of empty bottles strewn across the floor. They darted over to the bedside and applied what little first aid they knew, checking for the vital signs and placing the casualty in the recovery position. The porter grabbed the phone and called for an ambulance.

There was a sinister aspect to Jake McCullough's condition that caused an eerie silence. His colour was opalescent, his demeanour startling – bloated as if drowned. White skin with red-ringed eyes. Barely breathing.

During the fifteen or twenty minutes it took the ambulance to arrive, staff blocked the doorway to screen the scene from other guests. Busboys formed a defensive wall, their bare arms folded across crisp cotton shirts, necks craning to glimpse the first sign of death.

By now a small crowd had formed behind them in the corridor, jostling on tiptoe for a better view. Despite the staff's best efforts to maintain a sense of normality, the residents of nearby rooms had detected trouble. The arrival of two paramedics confirmed their suspicions.

Jake was lifted onto a stretcher and wheeled away to the drone of hoovering and the chattering of chambermaids further along the landing. His room would soon be cleaned too, and all traces of his stay removed. With Jake gone, the ebb and flow of human traffic resumed its mid-morning tempo on the flock-papered corridors of the Royal Pavilion Hotel. By lunchtime Jake's residency was but a dim memory stuffed into a black bin bag.

Jake McCullough's wife endured an anxious drive from London, made more miserable by the constant rain. By the time she arrived at the hospital in Brighton, Jake had been in intensive care for nearly three hours. It was no longer than three and a half hours since he had been found comatose in his hotel room. It was fortunate that he had been brought into hospital so promptly, the staff assured her, but she didn't hear them.

She had been preparing supper when she first received the news – brandishing a blunt knife in close combat with a variety of unwilling ingredients. Cooking wasn't her favourite occupation by a long chalk. She had been cursing her domestic lot whilst massaging a green salad and daydreaming up a quandary about Jake. *What to do about Jake?* It had become her life's quest – a battle she couldn't win; but she would never surrender. The frustration of her situation brought on tears. The massage became a strangulation; the salad leaves were limp when she had wanted them fluffy. Then the doorbell rang.

To her surprise she opened the door to find a man dressed in a replica football strip and dripping sweat onto her doorstep. She had a dim recollection of his face from a party or the pub or somewhere, but didn't recognise him immediately with his kit on. In his shorts he looked like a mutant. A strange man-child.

Jake was in hospital, he said breathlessly. He had been taken ill in Brighton, he said; it wasn't anything to worry about, he said; but he had been called on his mobile by Jake's agent, who suggested he take her straight down to the Casualty department at the Brighton Royal Infirmary so that she could be with him, he said; but still, there was nothing to worry about, he said. Then there was silence.

The news didn't shock her at first, but then she had a nagging feeling that things were worse than the footballer was suggesting.

Despite the developing pandemonium, she had the presence of mind to turn off the potatoes, put the salad in the fridge and take the kids and dog round to the people next door before leaving for the hospital. She also remembered to set the house alarm. And then she found herself sitting in this man's car. Tom. *That's right. He's called Tom*, she thought.

And Tom doesn't speak to her – he's too nervous. And then he asks a mundane question like: "It's a bit nippy for the time of year, isn't it?" and then shuts up again, because he realises he shouldn't have bothered her with small talk. And he's embarrassed because he knows he smells of sweat, and is still sweating because he's just been playing five-a-side football, and knows the smell isn't great, and curses under his breath when he sees that the car windows are steaming up from the condensation rising from his shirt – a damp Arsenal 'away' strip.

And then she arrives at the hospital and it takes forever to find the unit, the ward, the doctor. There's noise, and a barrage of questions.

"Mrs McCullough?"

"Yes?"

"Has your husband been complaining of giddiness or headaches?"

"No."

"Does he suffer from fits? Is he epileptic?"

"No. Why?"

"Has he complained of nausea or of feeling faint?"

"No, not that I know of. Please tell me what's going on..."

"Come this way and I'll take you up to intensive care. I'm afraid your husband is none too well," the young male doctor said, employing regulation bedside manner, but lacking the experience to make the reassuring tone of his patter sound convincing.

As the young doctor spoke, Mrs McCullough could feel herself slipping into shock, compromising her ability to take an active part in the strangeness unfolding around her.

The doctor led her to a lift. They went up two floors. He then shepherded her through some swing doors and onto a ward. At the top of the corridor he stopped her and looked into her eyes.

"Your husband is very sick, Mrs McCullough. He has acute alcohol poisoning, which has led to cardiac arrest. He's comatose, but comfortable. We've taken steps to ensure that he won't be in any pain. At present he is stable."

The doctor paused, waiting for a reaction before continuing, wanting confirmation that she was taking on board the seriousness of the situation.

"Oh," was all she could think of saying. It sounded inadequate and strange.

The young man unsettled her. Momentarily she was struck by his boyish beauty, his colour, his mild manner.

"We don't know if he is brain-damaged, but there is a probability factor."

Probability factor? she thought. *What the hell does that mean?*

"Oh," she heard herself saying again, in the same vacuous tone. It was a voice she didn't recognise as her own. "But he will be all right? It's not that bad?"

"Mrs McCullough, I'm afraid that it's very bad."

"Oh."

Her lack of reaction – that she wasn't hysterical, weeping and wailing and pulling out clumps of her hair – encouraged the young doctor to relax and forget that the woman's natural allegiance was to the patient and not to him, and that she might react differently should he fluff his lines.

But Mrs McCullough stood out amongst those he had come across in the day-to-day madness of his hospital routine. Compared to most, she was glamorous. Compared to any, she was stunning. Demure, she reminded him of Princess Grace of Monaco – thick, golden hair slashed into a bob that curled round and accentuated her cheekbones. Olive skin with blazing blue eyes. Probably between thirty-three and thirty-five. Definitely mid-thirties. Too old for him, he thought. How sad that she might soon be a widow. But her composed acceptance of the facts to date empowered him, giving him the confidence to share his prognosis with more graphic detail and enthusiasm, as though it might encourage a friendship.

"I'll take you to him shortly, Mrs McCullough, but I must warn you that he is on a life-support machine for now."

"Oh."

"Mrs McCullough, the next twenty-four hours are crucial. If he responds to treatment there might be some hope, but I must caution you to prepare yourself for bad news."

She thought she'd had the bad news.

The doctor spoke in a soft voice whilst making a stab at a glum, worried expression, the awkwardness of which irritated her and left her feeling patronised.

"Please just take me to him," she sighed in resignation.

The young doctor led her down the corridor, his shoes squeaking against the shiny parquet flooring, legs jerking as if trying to disown the feet and creating the impression that he was stepping through treacle; she glided along beside him as if in a trance.

Jake's was a bare room large enough for four beds, but empty now save for his and its attendant screens and machines, the only sound the intermittent bleeping of the various monitors encircling him like high-tech standing stones. Jake had been placed on his back with his chest exposed and covered in a tangle of wires and tubes, giving him the appearance of a puppet tossed aside by a petulant child. He was motionless, looking cold and alien. Mrs McCullough was disturbed that already there was something distant about the body before her, which she struggled to identify as the husband she had lain with a few nights before.

The Jake McCullough she knew had firm features. A taut face with strong character. His eyes were normally a sparkling deep blue that easily entranced the gullible. Yet now they were shut, and without them his face lost its authority, was devoid of personality. The only trace of the dashing blue eyes was a vague hint of them as they rolled under the eyelids tight against the skin, like the kicking feet of an unborn child.

Mrs McCullough sat down at the bedside, irritated that when she reached for his hand she had to fight to avoid the spaghetti of tubes and wires. But it was a relief to find that his palm was warm and feel the blood pulsing through his wrist.

"What can I do?" she asked the doctor, unsure of what to say and knowing that there was nothing that she could really do, however desperate to help.

The young doctor walked around the bed to put his hand on her shoulder, not bothering to answer the question.

"Is there anybody I can call for you, Mrs McCullough?" he asked.

"Catherine."

"What's her number?"

"No, no... My name is Catherine. Cathy. Oh, and this is Jake."

"But is there anyone?"

"Oh... no. It's OK, thank you very much. I'm sure the man who picked me up has done all that."

Catherine McCullough sat with her husband for an hour. It was strange sitting with this thing so unlike Jake. Jake was a live wire – this thing, inert and corpse-like. Regardless, she tried to speak to the body from time to time, just in case it was conscious of the words and that they might be of comfort. She took care not to nag or bully and attempted to reinvent the tone of voice she might have used when they first met.

Whom, if anybody, should she bring to his bedside to wake him from his coma? Which celebrity's voice would get through to Jake McCullough and bring him round? She could think of no one. Maybe the recording of Richard Burton reading *Under Milk Wood*, but then that was too melancholy; she didn't want to make his condition worse. And then, not being able to think of a favourite voice or piece of music that would stimulate him made her wonder if she had known him at all.

The hours passed by with the slowness of a schoolroom clock. She remembered double Physics on a Friday afternoon. Eyes fixed to the clock on the laboratory wall, impatient for the hands to wave out 5pm – the end of the school week. Free at last.

Before long familiar faces appeared on the ward bearing frowns. Jake's sisters arrived first.

"You go downstairs to the canteen, Catherine, and we'll sit with him. You need a break. Off you go. I'll stay here and Sinéad will go with you, if you like. Go on... Don't worry. I'll be with him. I'll fetch you if there's any change. Go on... Go and have a cup of coffee. It'll do you good. Go on..," Jake's older sister, Orla, urged. But Catherine wouldn't be swept away like a dead leaf when she knew she should be an oak.

She stayed through the night at the bedside. There was nothing to do, but she didn't think that she should sleep and when she did it was a catnap from which she was continually disturbed as her head bobbed forward with a jerk. The pace of events was unnerving. Every time she looked at Jake his condition was no better and with every passing second, minute and hour, he looked less like himself. It seemed odd that the last time she had seen him, he was bounding out of the house, excited about the awards dinner in Brighton. This was a strange way to see such an energetic person, only thirty-five for God's sake. He had always appeared indestructible. Could get away with murder. Gifted with outrageous fortune. The life and soul of the party. If he were to die it would seem immoral – as though the natural order of things had been overturned.

At around four o'clock in the morning, when Catherine was feeling so delirious through lack of sleep that she wondered if Jake's condition might be contagious, she thought she saw a movement, a slight flickering of his eyelashes. She was certain she'd seen something. Surely his hand had just moved? Then she fell asleep in her chair.

Come the morning, nothing had changed: Jake still lay prostrate; the machines still bleeped and blurred; nurses interrupted the solitude of their room at regular intervals to check on him and offer her cups of tea or coffee. Events appeared to have become dominated by a familiar routine that promised no change and offered little hope. Before long the young doctor returned, calmer and more self-assured. She wasn't sure if this should be interpreted as contempt.

"There's no improvement, Mrs McCullough," he said, but she already knew.

"I think you should go home and get some rest. Why don't you collect a few things together before coming back in? Don't worry, we'll call you if there's any change."

"Can you tell me anything more about his condition?"

"It's too early. If you come back in this afternoon, I might have some news for you then."

She turned to leave, touching her husband's hand as she did so – recoiling when she found that his flesh had grown cold and clammy.

Catherine McCullough took a cab back to London. *Sod the expense*, she thought. She dozed most of the way and would have slept but for the driver's insistence on making casual conversation. His was a persistent chitterchatter – irritating and impossible to ignore.

To excuse herself she called the children on her mobile. They had stayed over with the neighbour, who had kids of a similar age. The children, a girl of eight and a boy of six, were oblivious to the perilous condition of their father. They didn't detect the fear in their mother's voice.

The neighbour insisted on keeping the children until Catherine was ready to take them to the hospital. She was too tired to resist the offer. As soon as she got home, she slept.

Catherine didn't know how long she had been sleeping when the telephone woke her. It had invaded her dream – a vivid dream of Jake and herself as they were when they first met, in love and picnicking in a field in summer.

Catherine tried to ignore the ringing, but it persisted, rousing her until fully awake. Then, aware of the implications, she darted across the bedroom floor to lift the handset before the ringing stopped. As she seized the receiver she stubbed her toe. It was all she could do to stop herself from swearing with the pain as she put the phone to her ear. It was the hospital. Jake's condition was deteriorating, and she should come back without delay. In tears, Catherine called another cab and made the hellish journey back to Brighton.

At the hospital a sprinkling of friends and relatives was waiting outside Jake's room. More black looks.

"It won't be long," the young doctor whispered. And although she had been expecting this, the words still came as a shock.

The doctor led her into intensive care. Catherine was repulsed by the smell. A strange heavy odour like camphor or old meat – it reminded her of her grandmother's wardrobe and the smell of mothballs. Is that what they had planned for Jake? To preserve him in mothballs? It scared her when she realised that it was more likely the smell of decaying flesh – the scent of death.

Catherine sat holding her husband's hand, and watched as what life there remained in him drained away on his breath. It was a helpless situation with a slow unwinding inevitability. She could feel herself letting him go, little by little, as the gaps between breaths grew longer and shallower. His breathing seemed to sink further and further into his chest, deep into his diaphragm where it rattled with an alarming dry gurgling sound. The young doctor stood leaning over from the opposite side of the bed, attached to Jake by stethoscope. It was the doctor, she thought, who had become Jake's intimate. She was no more than a bystander now.

Meanwhile Catherine was unaware of the entrance of a small black figure whom she only noticed when he knelt down to pray at the foot of the bed. The priest's presence, ominous and unannounced, made her jump. Even though an absolution was required by Jake's religion, she didn't imagine it was required by Jake. She would have liked to send the priest packing, but already felt captive to events. The priest, sensing her discomfort, paused to reassure her by squeezing her wrist before resuming his prayers.

There was a pause in Jake's shallow breathing followed by one deep breath, almost a gasp, that lasted longer than the others. And then silence. The doctor looked over to Catherine and nodded.

Catherine let her head fall forward into her hands bracing herself for an emotional outburst that didn't come. For the moment she sat composed and unmoved, surrounded by stillness. Though her senses were sickened by the smell, she warmed to the finality of the moment. The nightmare had ended.

Then came the storm. The *Hail Marys*, the incessant clatter of tongues and an irresistible torrent of advice. Already an undertaker had been called. Immediately Jake's older sister, Orla, took the undertaker to one side, keen to stage-manage the rites: the prayer vigil, the funeral, the wake.

Catherine watched, distant and detached.

Under normal circumstances Jake would have been brought home that night to be laid out by the undertaker. His relatives would arrive and the customary prayer vigil would begin. Unfortunately the events preceding Jake's death had been far from normal and a death certificate would not be forthcoming. Jake would remain in hospital a while yet.

Catherine's initial concern, however, was to concoct a rational explanation for her children as to why their father was dead.

3.

"For God's sake! Don't you understand what this means? They'll want him buried within three days."

"I do sympathise, Mrs McCullough, but there's really nothing I can do."

The young doctor placed a hand on Catherine's shoulder. She shrugged it off.

"This is going to devastate the family. He's a Catholic, you know. They have very strict ways of doing things."

"Look, I know you're upset, but you have to understand... there's absolutely no way a death certificate can be signed now without the coroner's consent. We, too, have strict ways of doing things... and, I'm afraid, the coroner will want an autopsy. It's the law."

"Sod the law! They'll try and say it was suicide, won't they?"

"No, not necessarily."

"Good. We're agreed then."

"No, but– "

"Look, once his family gets wind of this there'll be a riot."

"I'm afraid I can't help that, Mrs McCullough. The coroner will want to investigate his death."

"Why?"

"Look, I'm sorry, but I have to be frank– "

"Oh, you're talking about the bottles, aren't you?"

"He did have chronic alcohol poisoning."

"Yes, but– "

"Well, you must agree... the circumstances were 'out of the ordinary'. As I say, it's the law. The coroner has to request a post-mortem if there is the slightest element of doubt. It doesn't mean to say that they think anything was amiss, but they have to investigate. It's a process they have to go through."

"You see! They'll try and prove it was suicide. Don't you realise what that means for a Catholic, Doctor?"

"Look, Mrs McCullough, off the record, I expect the post-mortem will be inconclusive. It's just something they have to do before declaring the cause of death. It's a procedure. I mean, they'll even look to see if there was a third party involved– "

"That's absurd. He died of a heart attack."

"Exactly. If you ask me, I don't think you have anything to worry about. It's a procedure!"

"You still don't get it, do you? It's not *me* I'm worrying about... it's his family."

A row broke out the moment Jake was moved to the mortuary and the undertaker left the hospital with an empty box. His two brothers, back home in Derry, were threatening to fly out and cause mayhem. The London-based McCulloughs, suspicious of British bureaucracy and desperate to help speed things up, blockaded the mortuary in the hope of retrieving Jake's remains. Bedlam ensued. The police were called to lift the siege.

It was in the aftermath of the chaos that Ned Labinski showed up at the hospital.

"Jesus, Ned, I'm sorry..."

Catherine burst into tears when she caught sight of him walking down the corridor, his shoulders hunched and arms hanging limp. *Poor Ned*, she thought.

For all his years Ned Labinski looked no more than a boy – tall, thin and sallow, with thick dark hair. His clear complexion hinted at innocence, his physique, frail, so that his clothes hung off him like hand-me-downs. POW chic. Plenty of room for growth. He had the scarecrow gait of a high jumper, but without the athleticism.

"Hey, it's OK!" Ned sobbed through a forced smile.

He stepped forward, swamping Catherine in the folds of his voluminous coat.

"Jesus, Ned, you'll miss him. He loved you so much, you know."

Ned pursed his lips and released a sigh to clear the snot and tears, then was self-conscious that the sigh might signal a form of tacit agreement too vainglorious for the moment. He wanted to get it right, spare her feelings, but the news had left him disoriented.

Catherine held him close, drawing strength from the physicality. Giddy, Ned stepped back and, grasping her hands, pulled her down beside him on the interlocking plastic chairs lining the corridor.

"Do you want to see him, Ned?"

"No thanks."

"Sure?"

"Oh God... I couldn't."

"Look, I'm going home shortly. Will you come? I need company."

Catherine and Ned escaped the scrum of people at the hospital. It was a welcome release, but Catherine in particular knew that it would be a temporary reprieve. They would have to deal with the coroner as soon as possible in order to get him to move on the post-mortem. With luck, the doctor had told her, she might get possession of Jake's body by the end of the week.

It was early evening. They caught a cab at the front steps and headed back to Finchley. The traffic on the M25 crawled even though the rush hour was long over. Catherine slept most of the way this time, relieved that when she awoke the cab was already pulling up at her house.

It was unnerving to be back at home surrounded by so many reminders of her life with Jake. It was also very quiet without the kids and the dog for company. She couldn't stop thinking about the terrible chores to come that would prolong her grief. She wasn't looking forward to having to sort through his stuff and couldn't bear the thought of having to throw anything away. But the house was warm, a relief after the cold sterility of the hospital ward and the icy cab. As soon as they got through the door, Catherine poured them a drink.

Ned had always loved the familiar smell of the house, imagining that it was some polish or cleaning agent they used, or maybe stale cigar smoke. It reminded him of his parents' home, and made him feel secure.

"Have you spoken to his mother?" Ned asked.

"Yeah... but only briefly."

"She'll want him brought home to Ireland, I suppose?"

"Oh God, yes, of course. It's what he would want too."

"Absolutely. I think he told me once, Cathy."

It seemed a betrayal to be talking about Jake in the past tense.

"Look, Ned. If you say he should go back, then he's going back."

"Well, I don't know, but he loved Northern Ireland."

"I wonder why he never married an Irish girl then, Ned?"

"Because he met you, silly."

"Ned, would you telephone the coroner for me tomorrow, and start letting our friends know?"

"Of course. It helps to stay busy."

"Everything's going to happen pretty quickly, Ned. Rightly or wrongly, Jake's relatives are going to have strong ideas about how things should be done over the next couple of days. How he's going to be buried, where, which church and all that. If you've got any thoughts on the matter, I think you should let me know pretty soon before we're completely overtaken by events. I mean, there's little doubt that the family will want him buried rather than cremated, they'll want a Catholic mass, they'll want a wake and they'll probably want an open coffin at the wake. But that's OK. We're not to get uptight about these things, Ned, because... well because... well you know– "

"Because he's dead?"

"Exactly," Catherine smiled. "Because he's dead."

4.

Charlie Clarke didn't like Mondays and this one had been no exception. Each Monday morning was the lid to a can of worms that he would rather not open. His working weeks were characterised by chaos. Self-employment had become a lonely and fraught existence.

Since the divorce, his income needed to be much higher than could be achieved by his earnings. Although his talent as an illustrator was much appreciated by his clients, his bank statements reminded him that his services were undervalued when it came to remuneration. He was, therefore, forced to take every job going in order to support the extravagant lifestyles that he and his ex-wife had carelessly become accustomed to.

There were times, scary times, when the work didn't come at all. But more often he worked too hard. It had already, in part, cost him a marriage, and was now threatening his health. His eyesight was a particular cause for concern.

Twelve years of running his own business from a box-like studio in Borough and Clarke still hadn't grasped the most basic of principles: that no amount of hard graft could compensate for a lack of organisation. He knew that he was dysfunctional, but thought that the ensuing confusion was like a badge of office to be proud of. He was an artist, after all. Artists suffer. The drudgery of the long hours lavished on illustrations for his diverse clientele, from book publishers to advertising agencies, was the penance he paid for living in a high-maintenance city.

"There's no substitute for hard work, you know. You'll never achieve anything without working for it. Hard work never killed anyone..."

His father's mantras had become etched on his psyche and drove him to further anxieties. That he had never bothered to rationalise his approach to work – though friends had often tried to counsel him on the subject, and though much of the pain was unnecessary – made him a martyr. But his stamina and will to battle on were indicative of an inner fortitude which, if wasted on his business, had ensured his survival. Just.

Mondays were an abomination, but a careful glance through the week ahead in his voluminous desk diary would have shown that he was attempting to complete the whole week's business in just one day, and that Monday's page was disproportionately weighed down with jobs, meetings and phone calls. If he had taken care to spread his agenda across the blank pages of the rest of the week, his life, and Mondays in particular, would take on a much more manageable pace. It was with some relief on the Monday evening therefore, that Clarke turned the key to his two-bedroom apartment in Battersea.

Six o'clock was early to be getting home. However, he had been away for the weekend and, having battled through the day with a force-nine hangover, was ready for the comforting blow of a large gin and tonic. He hoped he wouldn't find the apartment as untidy and shambolic as he remembered leaving it.

At home Clarke was a piles person. He didn't have the discipline to put things away, but was ordered enough to leave them in neat piles classified by size rather than by kind. Books tended to end up in the 'big' pile but could be joined by dirty plates and LPs. Socks and pants would end up in the 'small' pile, where they were often company for CDs and mail. There was little logic at work.

That the apartment was Edwardian helped, for many of the original features remained, including the fireplaces, cornicing, and sash windows, and however likely it was that some of the piles – those containing perishable food in particular – could become a threat to health, the general effect was not displeasing to the eye. It conjured up a relaxed ambience that bordered on the bohemian and was visitor friendly. His home could easily be mistaken for that of an eccentric professor.

As Clarke pushed the door open, the tranquillity of his flat was threatened by the phone ringing from the kitchen. He ignored it. Nothing was going to disturb his evening of relaxation.

After five rings the answerphone cut in. Retreat to the lounge seemed essential to escape the monotone of his own voice on the announcement tape, but he stopped short when he heard the drunken slurring of the caller:

"What about the bloody match... hey? We stuffed the bastards, Charlie? One bloody nil... hey? Give us a call sometime and we'll go out and get pissed... Just you and me... You and me... and we'll get absolutely rat-arsed..."

Clarke smiled – Northern Irish brogue, unbridled enthusiasm – the voice was unmistakably Jake McCullough's. *'The bloody match'* the cause of Clarke's hangover.

A call from Jake McCullough was a theatrical event and always welcome except at three in the morning when received from some seedy part of town. While Clarke would be asleep, McCullough would be as pissed as a newt and wanting to share his exuberance on the way back from the pub, club or party.

Until recently however, Clarke hadn't heard much from Jake. They had met on the art and design foundation course in Belfast and then gone on to London together to study for their degrees. An Irish Mafia, they had stayed close and looked out for one another. After college, when Jake became established as a writer, they drifted apart. Soon Jake married Catherine and moved to Devon, claiming the country air helped him 'create'. Clarke was sceptical. He couldn't imagine Jake being content in rural isolation, but the

McCulloughs stayed for ten years. There was little contact then, save the odd phone call and a card at Christmas.

Two years ago, Jake had moved back to London and re-established contact. He said he was looking for fresh inspiration. Clarke was relieved to have Jake back in circulation. He needed the company of an old friend after his divorce.

Both of them were Irish exiles of sorts. Jake was from Mid-Ulster; whereas Clarke's parents were emigres from Dublin. And although Clarke's South London accent didn't give much of a clue to his roots, he had been born in Dublin and still had an army of relatives on the Northside to support his credentials.

"Where the fuck are you, Charlie? Give us a call, mate..." Jake continued to slur into the phone.

Clarke let him finish his message without picking up the receiver. He would return the call later when he had got himself settled. First, he needed a drink to steady himself.

The evening drifted. Clarke felt uncomfortable that he had already dedicated so much of it to sitting in front of the telly rather than working on his pet project. The project – the writing and illustration of a children's book – had been invested with more hope than time of late.

"Get off your fat arse and do something useful for a change... Don't get caught on the ropes... get up and fight! Fight!" his father's words taunted. The work ethic burned hot.

"If we're Irish why don't we support Arsenal, Jake?"

Charlie and Jake shared a passion for football.

"Because we're Irish and not *Oirish*. We're not bloody bogtrotters, Clarkey. We're the Irish cognoscenti. Anyway, Arsenal are bloody boring."

"Yeah, but they're bloody good."

"Look, Chelsea are football chic. They're stylish and postmodern with a cutting edge."

"But they never win anything."

"Yes, but they are our team, Charlie – our chosen ones. We must follow our stars. And anyway, *Il destino... favours the brave*, as Zola might say."

"Emile Zola?"

"No, Gian-bloody-franco Zola: the country's favourite Italian socceroo, you berk."

"But anyway, we still never win anything... however brave we are."

"Wait, you'll see. We'll beat them come Sunday."

When Charlie and Jake had last talked, they planned a 'get-together' at a friend's house for the Sunday to watch Chelsea play Arsenal in the fourth round of the FA Cup. Unfortunately, Jake couldn't make it because of the awards dinner in Brighton. The rest gathered regardless.

Cans were opened early. Too early. By kick-off few could interpret the action of the first half as it unfolded before them on the TV. It was a dour game. Chelsea didn't play well and didn't look like winning. It mattered little to the house party, who in their intoxicated state had trouble concentrating on anything that wouldn't pour into a glass or couldn't be picked off a plate. They barely understood, therefore, the significance of the penalty awarded to Chelsea in the dying seconds of the match, and hardly noticed as the team's continental star drove the ball into the back of the net to bring about a most unlikely win for the home side. For Chelsea. One-nil. If the couch potatoes had been unable to follow the game, they were more than capable of celebrating the victory.

Before he got too lethargic and before it got too late, Clarke thought he would distract himself by returning Jake's call. It would be entertaining. They would wallow in the glory of their team's great victory.

Clarke tapped in Jake's mobile number from memory, wondering if he would still be as drunk as he sounded on the answerphone. Clarke thought about Jake's legendary drinking habit while the phone rang. Jake had told him recently that his friends were getting edgy about his drinking and had started to badger him with well-intentioned advice. Clarke had reassured Jake that what most people consider to be a serious drink problem in England would be no more than a harmless pastime back home in Ireland. But now he wondered.

There was no answer on Jake's mobile. Clarke couldn't be bothered to leave a message. He'd give it another go in the morning. Jake would be sober by then, too, and the conversation more fruitful.

Clarke had a quick shower – he hated baths – made another gin and tonic, got comfortable on the sofa and prepared to fall asleep in front of the television.

5.

If Clarke's Mondays were a mad scramble up a cliff face, then Tuesdays were a leisurely stroll across a meandering plain. Once Clarke had negotiated the drizzle and crazy South London traffic on his ancient Lambretta, he picked up a paper, a coffee and a roll; stripped off his waterproofs; rammed the Elgar *Cello Concerto* into the CD player and settled into his studio chair to enjoy the day's headlines before work.

The sports pages still screamed of the weekend's football. The coverage had changed from match-reporting of Chelsea's victory to post-mortems on Arsenal's defeat. It renewed Clarke's enthusiasm to share his triumphalism with Jake McCullough.

Jake's mobile didn't ring for long before it was answered by a familiar voice.

"Hello?"

"Good afternoon, Mrs McCullough, this is Finchley Council. We've had a rather nasty complaint about yer bins, now..."

Clarke hoped his Cork accent was convincing.

"Oh God, Charlie... It's you, isn't it?" Catherine sounded despondent. "You don't know, do you?"

"Know what?"

"He's dead, Charlie..."

A pause. Clarke dumbstruck.

"...Jake died this morning."

"*You what?*"

"He'd been drinking. Heavily. Very heavily. No one's really sure... But it may have been deliberate."

"What? *Jesus*, Catherine. What can I... I had no... He tried to phone me yesterday after... I was just returning his call... Is there anybody there with you? Where are you, for God's sake?"

"Finchley. I'm home. Ned's here... some of Jake's family... Oh Charlie, what the hell was he thinking? What about the children?"

"Look, I'll get off the line... Don't tell me any more, I'll get hold of Ned later. But you know if there's– "

"I know."

Clarke put the receiver down, bowing his head to stare across the layout pad before him. His eyes glazed over as they rested on the lake of milk-white paper. The news brought on claustrophobia like a black and menacing cloud. There was nothing to be done. The shock numbed.

Keep busy. He was sure if he got busy right away then the grieving could be avoided for a while. Be practical, he told himself. Be practical. Then he sat for twenty minutes trying to contemplate the world without Jake and trying to imagine Catherine's terrible sadness. What to do next? How to react? He wished there was someone he could hug.

Why the hell hadn't he picked up the phone when Jake called? Clarke blinked to release the tears gathering in his eyes. A bead rolled down each cheek, then a trickle. It was surprisingly easy to make himself cry. He watched as the tears spread out in big blotches across his layout pad. The splash marks were quite beautiful. A subtle watercolour. After a few minutes, when the tears came no more, he shook his head to clear it and regain his composure. Be practical, he kept thinking. Be practical.

Clarke called Finchley. To his relief Ned answered the phone.

Ned and Clarke had been friends at art college, but hadn't been in touch much since. They probably hadn't had a conversation of any consequence for years. By now Clarke couldn't remember how well he had ever known him. He could recall being invited to some of Ned's first private views, but after that? It all seemed so long ago. Clarke was sure however, that of the two of them, Ned had stayed closer to Jake since college. Ned and Jake were inseparable from the day they met. Some said that they were like husband and wife. There was much that they had in common. They had both gravitated towards writing: Ned was now a Features Editor on one of the weekend supplements. They shared the same interests, the same friends, were physically similar: both were of tall, dark and handsome stock. But in personality they were opposites, Ned gentle and shy, Jake loud and extrovert. Ned, however, was the only one of the friends capable of curbing Jake's more excessive behaviour. They made a good double act.

"Hello Charlie," Ned murmured.

He was unsure how friendly to be under the circumstances.

"Ned, how are you?" Clarke cringed at the inanity of his question. "Er... I'm just phoning to offer my help."

"There's not much you can do really, Charlie."

"I could let people know, if you like. It might keep them out of your hair for a while."

"Maybe... Yes, I guess that would be helpful."

"Do you need me over there, Ned?"

"Not now. Maybe later, Charlie. The place is crawling at the moment. But yes... if you could let people know what's happened, that'd be a great help."

"How's Cathy, Ned?"

"She's amazing at the moment, you know. She's got to be really... for the kids. How much has she told you?"

"Not a lot. I didn't know anything until I called earlier. Actually, he tried calling me last night. He left a message on the answerphone. I was returning his call when Catherine gave me the news."

"Yeah, he tried calling me. Fuck! I missed his call too. Look, Charlie, you might as well know... it was drink. I don't want to go into detail, but basically he went a bit overboard at the awards dinner. He had a heart attack, for God's sake. By the time they found him there was little that could be done. He was taken straight into emergency. He died overnight."

"Jesus, Ned. And do *you* think he– "

"Did it intentionally? Well... yes, actually. He wasn't a very happy bunny, Charlie. Apparently his blood/alcohol level was shocking. Anyway, look, if you really want to help, just telephone as many people as you can and let them know."

"What if they ask about the funeral?"

"Just tell them that it's more than likely going to be at the weekend. We won't know for sure until the coroner's happy. Mind you, I don't know how many will go if it's in Northern Ireland."

"Right. Where do I start?"

"I don't know. Just phone anyone you can think of. Start with our college friends. Oh, and by the way, Charlie, whenever the funeral is, and if you can make it, Cathy wants you to say a few words."

"What? At the funeral?"

"Yes. A eulogy."

"Oh God... I don't think so, Ned. I mean you're the guy's best friend."

"No. I don't want to. I couldn't. Besides, you're Irish. No one would understand me."

"What's being Irish got to do with anything? Jesus, aren't we all Irish, Ned? I had an English granny. I bet you've got an Irish one."

"Actually, Charlie, all my ancestors were Polish Jews... Labinskis."

"Yeah, well. We'll see," Clarke mumbled evasively. "Ned, is it all right if I come up to Finchley later? I'd like to see Catherine."

"Sure, but phone me on my mobile first, OK? You've got the number?"

Clarke put the receiver down with a sigh, looked around his studio and wondered if he could possibly tackle any of the work that needed to be done in his present state of mind, shocked and unsure how to react: whether to be sympathetic or angry.

He had a love/hate relationship with his studio depending on whether he wanted to be there (because he was enjoying a project) or had to be there (because of his bank balance). Its saving grace was the wall-to-ceiling window at the gable end which beckoned in light throughout the year. Every surface of the boxy room was covered in a heavy snowfall of paper – the detritus of jobs past, mixed with the rough working drawings of commissions in progress.

Tuesday was fast descending into the manic farce usually the preserve of Monday. Clarke switched off his Apple Mac, put down his pen, got out his address book, and started dialling.

As his fingers punched in the first phone number that seemed relevant, Clarke agonised over the best way to break the news. How do you tell your old friend's best friends, whom you haven't seen for years, that the best friend is dead, and worse, that it might have been suicide? Clarke decided that the only way to handle the call was to be as dispassionate as possible. He visualised himself talking with the precise pronunciation of a newsreader – detached and deadpan.

"Hello Sarah. It's Charles Clarke."

They hadn't talked in eight years.

"Christ, Charlie! What the hell are you calling me for?"

"It's about Jake."

"What's the silly fool up to now?"

"Actually Sarah, it's bad news. I'm afraid. Jake died last night."

"Oh my God, Charlie... I didn't... I mean... How? What happened?"

"A heart attack."

"Fucking hell, Charlie. A heart attack... at his age?"

"Well, I don't know much, but Catherine says that it had something to do with drink."

Clarke knew there was no point in hiding the truth. The facts would be known sooner or later. Catherine would prefer that people just knew what there was to be known, without any pussyfooting.

The telephoning was cathartic; it not only kept Clarke occupied, but also helped him to come to terms with the reality of Jake's death by forcing him to talk about it repeatedly. Many of the friends appeared to know much more about Jake of late than he, especially about his drinking. It made Clarke self-conscious – that maybe he was underqualified to be doing the job. They might wonder why the hell *he* had taken it upon himself to be calling *them* with the news. But it wasn't the time to be too self-reflective.

A difficult call was to Jake's girlfriend from their college days. The two years the relationship lasted felt like a lifetime then. The girl, Loulou McCall, was Jake's first serious girlfriend. Clarke smiled when he pictured her fractious temperament fuelled on drink.

Jake and Loulou had moved in together in the second year. They had had a whirlwind romance. And although the whirlwind grew tempestuous towards the end, they remained close friends in its wake. They were like brother and sister. There was a bond and mutual understanding that never quite left them.

Clarke hadn't spoken to her for two or three years. Not since her move to Paris. Unfortunately, he only had a work number, scribbled onto a tatty scrap of newspaper. Nervous, he dialled the number. She answered. He hoped she might have heard about Jake already. She hadn't. But Clarke had had plenty of practice breaking the news.

"I can't believe he would do that," Louise McCall responded in a high-pitched voice, once mellow, now a screech. "Jesus, poor Jake. I would never have thought... He *was* a bit mixed up, though."

"What do you mean mixed up?"

"Oh, nothing really."

"What?"

"Nothing..." she replied, defiant. "I only saw him two weeks ago, Charlie."

"Really?"

"Yeah. He made a point of taking me out to lunch when I was in town. I hadn't seen him for a while."

"Really?"

"Maybe he was saying goodbye," she mumbled as if thinking aloud. "But then, you know, he appeared perfectly happy. Mind you, he was as pissed as a fart. We both were."

"What did you mean when you said he was a bit mixed up?"

"Oh nothing. He had his fair share of problems, though."

"Yeah... but what were they? You lived with him. You should know."

"Jesus, that was a lifetime ago."

"Yeah, but still– "

"Oh... I don't know if I want to say right now, actually."

"OK... OK... Will you be going to the funeral, Loulou?"

"Certainly. If I can."

"Is that a yes or a no?"

"If I can," she repeated firmly.

"Look, I'll talk to you nearer the time. If you want any more details, just call... We'll talk again."

A couple of hours on the phone, chasing telephone numbers and contacting Jake's friends, and Clarke thought he had the task done, the grapevine activated. Some of the conversations provided Clarke with graphic titbits which, like the edges of a jigsaw, fitted neatly into place. Many more threw up obscure pieces that, like clear blue sky, were hard to place and added little detail to the overall picture. When Clarke returned to his work, he found himself panicking – worried that if he couldn't make some headway soon, then he wouldn't be able to attend the funeral.

Between six and seven, dusk began filling the large window with twilight. Clarke pulled the studio door shut, cursing under his breath when he caught a last glimpse of the workload being left behind, and hoping that the next day might prove more productive.

Outside in the rain, he wrestled with the old Lambretta to rock it off its centre stand. The scooter was wet and slippery and heavy. A sumo mismatch, the bike toppled over, slipping from his grasp and skewing slowly into a puddle. A purple mist descended.

"*Bastard, bastard!*" Clarke shouted, kicking out at the tank.

6.

Mr Smith and Mr Collins, mortuary attendants working deep in the bowels of the Brighton Royal Infirmary, knew little of the personalities of the people who passed through their hands. They didn't care to. The naked bodies stored in the artificially chilled atmosphere of the mortuary remained anonymous to them both. The two middle-aged men preferred it that way. They agreed that it didn't 'do' to get too well acquainted with their guests. They therefore maintained a formal and professional detachment at all times.

Their work was difficult and not best suited to those of a squeamish disposition. The nature of their work forced upon them a more intimate knowledge of their visitors' physical characteristics than they would normally have desired. Over the years in the mortuary's clinically controlled environment, therefore, they had become inured to the shock. They had learned to suppress their emotions. It showed in their blank expressions and understated body language. They had become cold fish.

When the pathologist – he of a different tribe, a 'white coat' – came smiling into the mortuary and Smith and Collins were required to assist by handling those bodies that were of specific interest to him – those that were mauled, mangled or mashed out of their normal form – they were hasty about their work. The less said the better. Their detachment was tested.

So far, in long and demanding careers, they had been lucky. Only once did they pull back the covering shroud to discover a corpse that was known to them. Both holding a corner of the orange sheet, they looked at each other for acknowledgement, nodding in agreement that this indeed was Mr Smith's nephew, Phillip. A car crash. Very nasty. Through the windscreen. Not a pleasant sight.

In tandem and with the timing of synchronised swimmers – unsmiling – they looked down at the young man's swollen features, looked back up into each other's eyes, nodded again, and replaced the cover without speaking.

Nodding was their language. They rarely spoke. A life lived behind a surgical mask had muffled their voices. When they did speak it was when the work necessitated that one ask the other for a certain implement or tool, but even then they understood which implement and which tool by the type of nod and its direction.

For nearly thirty years they had drifted around the mortuary in their brown laboratory coats like middle-aged mime artists, by now handling the dead with the deftness and gentle touch of antiquarian book dealers.

Years of lifting, wheeling and leaning over bodies had encouraged a slight curvature in their spines, which became more pronounced the longer they stood at their work. Like a pair of badly sprung Anglepoise lamps, they stooped over the deceased, each fixed in a rigid pose from which they could never fully straighten. They had become a matching pair.

Despite the men's emotional detachment there was much they could tell about each of the guests passing through their hands by observing their physical appearance. The two had learned much about people from the years spent looking at naked corpses and as a result could interpret the most subtle of marks and bruises, wrinkles and lines, scars and blemishes. There were telltale characteristics within the general wear and tear that gave many clues to the visitor's status in life, their income, the quality of their lives, whether they had been hardworking, and about their indulgences and overindulgences.

Jake's teeth made a deep impression on Smith and Collins – they alone told them much of his story: they told them he was affluent; they told them he had been successful overseas, probably in America. The bridge work alone suggested California and hinted at a five-figure investment from at least a six-figure income. Probably a non-smoker, but prone to lapses.

His hands were manicured, his toenails too. His hair was well cut – long but not unkempt. His skin was tanned, not too deep, just enough to conceal the North European pallor. Judging by his paunch-to-age ratio, he was probably a thirtysomething who liked to live a little, but who hadn't let himself go completely. His muscle tone was reasonable – he obviously did just enough to keep himself fit. He was possibly a vain man.

These traits were familiar to Smith and Collins, the marks of the middle classes, the comfortably well off. If Smith and Collins cared to hazard a guess, they would agree that he was in business, probably his own, possibly involved in the entertainment industry or the arts.

If they had been more curious, the two men might have wondered why this thirtysomething male was visiting them in the mortuary so prematurely. But they weren't in the slightest bit curious, and chose not to care. They didn't read his case notes. Here was nothing new or out of the ordinary.

Mr McCullough was but one of a hundred visitors that year. He was therefore dealt with in the same precise and professional manner, without fuss or ceremony, and stored away in one of the many oven-like cupboards, whose round and black enamel doors punctuated the sterile white tiles on the back wall of the mortuary. Jake would lie there to await the dissecting skills of the pathologist in the morning.

7.

Sinéad McCullough sat staring into her coffee. The cup was half empty and the drink getting cold. A memory flashed back from her childhood to disturb her daydreaming – of sitting in the kitchen of the old house and spotting a skin on her coffee as it cooled. Her mother would be begged to scoop it off with a teaspoon. The thought made her shiver. She hated the taste with the revulsion an arachnophobc feels for spiders. Sinéad couldn't remember the last time she had seen skin on coffee; it didn't seem to happen any more. Ever.

She was perched on a stool at the breakfast bar in Jake's house in Finchley, having volunteered to mind the children for a few days. She missed the support of her older sister Orla, who had flown home to Derry to comfort Breige, their mother. Within the next day or so the two of them were planning to travel over to London, as Breige was insistent on being party to the funeral preparations at the earliest opportunity.

From time to time Sinéad looked up to observe Catherine and Ned through the glass of the kitchen door. They were sitting on the sofa in the living room, talking. She strained to hear what they were saying, their voices muffled by the glass. When they got excited she could make out words, phrases, even whole sentences, but nothing that made sense. The detachment irked her. They had been distancing themselves all day. They were being 'terribly nice' and considerate, but excluding her from the intimacy of their conversations. And although she was aware that the babysitting was vital in that it would take the pressure off Catherine, she too was grieving and needed adult company.

The news about Jake had been a terrible blow to Sinéad. With the sudden loss came a gradual realisation that she had taken her brother for granted. He had always seemed a permanent fixture in her life. But as she sipped the lukewarm coffee, it now occurred to her that she had been conned, that Jake had presented a facade, a contrived impression that he was in control, strong and resilient. The Jake she had loved was an invention, a character more befitting a homely soap opera: a John-Boy Walton. The reality hurt. For all that she had loved him, she now realised that she had barely known him at all. He had never revealed that there were problems.

A wince crossed her face with ugly lines. She tried to think of lighter things, turning to look for the children through the kitchen window. They had been playing in the shed at the far end of the garden, running in and out of the rain, oblivious to the angst that had enveloped the adults. Now, however, they were sitting opposite one another on their haunches just inside the door, and petting the dog. Their mood appeared to have changed. Maybe they were more aware than she gave them credit for. She resisted the temptation to call out to them, leaving them to their deliberations.

Subtle movement from the sitting room caught her eye. She watched as Catherine took Ned's hand and rubbed the back of it with her palm. Sinéad couldn't make out who was comforting whom. She picked up her coffee, and then nearly dropped the cup when she spotted a thick yellowing skin.

"Look, Cathy... does anybody really know? It's obvious, isn't it? I mean you can't choose who you're going to fall in love with. It's not like picking fruit. OK, so sure, maybe some people do, and maybe that works for them, but where's the passion in that?

Where's the romance? When you fall in love with someone, you just fall in love... Bang! It's that simple. And is that so wrong?"

"I know, I know... but that's not what I am saying, Ned."

"Oh, I don't know. It's just that everybody else seems to think that relationships can be contrived, that it's *simple*, that life is that *simple*. Sure, life can be very simple for some. If you stick to a precise routine, live in the street you were born in, mix with the same people, marry your childhood sweetheart... and sure, you will be very safe... but you might as well live in a prison if all you want in life is security. Christ, the world's not that big, Cathy. You might as well get out and walk about a bit and see what's there... try a few things out. And that's what he did. He liked to explore."

"That's fine for him, Ned... but what about us? What about the children? What about *their* needs? Anyway, it didn't do him much good in the end, did it? He obviously wasn't very happy."

"That wasn't totally his fault. The thing is, he tried."

"I don't know, Ned. The kids and I just needed a little continuity. I know he had a tough time in the last year or two– "

"He totally lost the plot."

"Exactly, and where does that leave the kids? He had a responsibility to them. They didn't deserve this, Ned. They didn't deserve for him to lose the plot."

"No, you're right, but... Oh, I don't know. It's just that he was too clever to surrender to normality... it... it..."

"What?"

"I was going to say 'it would probably have killed him', but then again, it obviously did. Maybe it was the level of expectation... ethics... scruples... principles... I think it all drove him a little mad."

"It certainly didn't get easier for him," Catherine sighed.

Conversation with Ned came easily. Of all the people who had been busying around her that day, he was the only one whom Catherine felt she could take into her confidence. He was the only one who knew Jake as well as she. For that, she respected him, and also because she knew that other than the children and herself, Ned was the only one whom Jake had loved.

"It's terrible, Ned, tonight I feel more relaxed than I have for months. Jake's behaviour has been bloody awful recently. His drinking's got worse and his behaviour unpredictable. To tell you the truth, he's been hell to live with for over a year now. You know he's always been mad about the kids, well recently he's been very hard on them… impatient, irritable – he's had them in tears."

"Jesus, I'm sorry, I didn't have a clue."

"You know, the really sad thing is that they seem calmer, too. It's probably because they don't have to worry any more about saying or doing something that might drive Jake into a temper or to the pub for the night."

"No. Really?"

"Well, you see, he'd taken to staying out until one or two in the morning, coming home steaming and falling around the house while we tried to sleep. It was bloody frightening. At least now there's some peace. The children seem more relaxed."

Catherine shrugged. Thoughts and impressions were coming to her in loops and spins and making her giddy. At one moment she felt huge remorse, at the next, relief. She couldn't see a straight path to follow. And now she felt ashamed to suggest that, like her, her children might feel relief.

But she was determined to survive this, determined to reclaim her life. Jake had overwhelmed her; his was a large ego to live with. Having swept her off her feet when they first met, he had been letting her down to earth with the hardest of bumps ever since. Having been so devoted to him, and so wrapped up in their domestic life, she hadn't been aware of any deterioration in their relationship. However, it had happened, slowly and inexorably, until the fight was lost. She resented him for his part in their defeat.

Time was on her side, however. She was still only thirty-four. A young and attractive thirty-four. Her hair still had its rich colour, her blue eyes still sparkled, her skin was still taut and unlined, and her figure still firm. She hadn't lost her smile. As Jake had drunk more, she had drunk less. As he had grown more angry and embittered, she had stayed focused and objective. The pilot light of her spirit still burned. Since she had survived life with him, she could survive his death.

"It's funny, you know, he was so carefree when he was younger."

"You mean, before he met me, Ned?"

"No, silly. I just think as he got older he got a little disappointed. I think he finally realised that the world was round after all."

"He did like to break the rules... to lead the revolution."

"I think he thought of himself as a conscientious objector... a war poet... a Sassoon."

"Hairdressing *is* hell– "

"Maybe more of a flouter than a revolutionary."

"True. There haven't been too many revolutionaries that play golf."

"Jesus, Catherine. What was it with Jake and golf? I mean he liked to be unconventional... but to play *golf*?"

"He claimed it was an Irish thing."

"What? Like drinking Guinness and Irish dancing?"

"Well, just that golf has a different culture there. You know... It's not so much a preserve of the middle classes. Not so jacket and tie."

"Well, I could never understand it. At least he didn't wear a Pringle sweater and canary-yellow slacks."

"Actually, he was rather proud of a navy V-neck with a Royal Portrush Golf Club crest on it. I think he found it in a locker room somewhere in Surrey," Catherine said, smiling.

"Now I think about it actually, Che Guevara played golf. I saw an old black-and-white photo of him on the cover of the *Sunday Times Magazine* a couple of years ago swinging a golf club in a beret, combat boots and army fatigues."

"And Alice Cooper's supposed to be very keen. And Iggy Pop."

"Yeah... and David Cassidy... they all play together."

In the kitchen the muffled words from the lounge tested Sinéad McCullough's patience. She grew even more irritated when she saw Ned and Catherine laughing. Although she knew that laughter wasn't a bad thing, it unnerved her and made her feel excluded. Their mood was different to hers. *She* felt no joy.

54

8.

A doorbell rings. A short polite ring followed by a pause, and then another ring, but more urgent. Eventually there is movement. The letter box is pushed up from inside the house allowing light to dart out and cast a yellow glow on the figure waiting outside. The letter box sprouts tremulous fingertips, then quivering lips.

"You'll have to come round the back, Charlie! I'm really sorry, but I can't find the key to the sodding deadlock. I think the effing dog's had it again," the letter box cried.

Clarke fumbled through the foliage, trying to find the path leading to the back door, his feet scrunching on the gravel – the only means of navigation in the dark and pouring rain. At least this time he would get access by a door – the last time he visited the McCulloughs' it was gained through a window, the dog having buried both sets of keys.

The house was silent. Friends and relatives had long been persuaded to leave. Even Ned had gone home to gather up some clothes and relax for a while. Catherine only had Jake's sister Sinéad for company.

The house, a big postmodern sixties block, white and featureless, reminded Clarke of the hacienda-style sprawl polluting the coastline of Donegal. Though immaculate, the house had its eccentricities. The toaster, for instance, needed a smack to persuade it to toast, the TV remote required repeated slaps before it would change channels, light switches and pull cords needed sharp tugs or gentle teasing, taps dripped and radiators leaked. There was a knack to everything, an eccentricity that mirrored the characteristics of the occupants. Perhaps it's not only dogs that resemble their owners, Clarke thought.

The last time he had been at the Finchley house was for a dinner party in the summer. It didn't go well. He arrived half an hour late, unaccompanied and shy. The other guests intimidated him from the first polite handshake. There were two couples – opinionated young professionals. It surprised Clarke how ambivalent Jake was towards their claptrap, especially when the conversation turned to Northern Ireland. But then Jake had appeared pretty far gone – too far gone. So far gone he fell asleep, face down in his dessert.

"Catherine..," Clarke mumbled, giving her a tender hug; detecting the scent of wine on her breath.

She hadn't changed, physically. Nothing, it seemed, could compromise the vigour of her beauty.

"Oh, I'm so sorry, Charlie. He was very, very fond of you, you know."

She poured him a glass of dry white, determined to appear relaxed.

"You know Sinéad, don't you, Charlie?"

"Of course."

Clarke gave Sinéad a small kiss on the cheek as she stood up to greet him. It was reassuring to see Sinéad. Like many who had passed through the house that day, Clarke was wary of being with Catherine on his own in case he said something stupid to upset her.

Sinéad, the baby of the McCullough family, still seemed very youthful, even though she was probably in her late twenties by now. Clarke had always found her dark looks attractive. She was a typical raven-haired Derry girl with dark brown eyes and black curly hair – thick like strong rope. A great mass of it. And yet despite her striking appearance she had always seemed so serene and inviolable. A little Virgin Mary. A chain-smoking Virgin Mary in denim. As usual he found himself tongue-tied in her presence.

He smiled awkwardly at Sinéad, feeling foolish in his waterproofs, which made slithery swishing noises as he waddled across the kitchen, anointing the furniture with raindrops. He imagined he looked like an oversized baby in a giant romper suit.

"Come in and we'll dry that stuff off."

Clarke followed Catherine across the room. He was nervous of her. Though quiet, she seemed very focused, strangely so, as though she had become charged with some supernatural power. But then the emotional burden she was carrying for her children was such that she needed to be strong.

"Have you had any sleep yet, Catherine?"

Clarke sat down to face her across the breakfast bar, feeling exposed beneath the brightness of the kitchen spotlights.

"Don't worry. I'll get plenty tonight."

"Good, good..." Clarke said, looking down at his threadbare socks and lost for words.

"Charlie, will you be coming to the funeral?"

"Of course."

"Right, will you do something for me, then? Well, for Jake too, actually."

He looked up from the hole he had discovered in the left sock.

"You want me to say a few words for Jake at the funeral, don't you?"

"Well yes– "

"Ned mentioned it, but I don't think it should be me."

"Bollocks, Charlie."

Clarke was taken aback by her bluntness.

"Well, what about Ned?" he asked, tentatively.

"Ned's suffered a big loss. You know how close they were. Ned's such a big softy, Charlie. I'm worried about him. I really don't know how he's going to cope with the funeral. He's under enough pressure without having to worry about making a bloody speech, or whatever. Knowing Ned, he'd cry all the way through. He'd hate that."

"That's all very well, Catherine, but I have to be honest with you... I might have known Jake for a long time, but I don't feel I really knew him that well. Especially over the last nine or ten years. You know we hadn't been in touch much until recently."

"That's very honest of you, Charlie. But, no. You should do it because it's what he would have wanted. I want you to. Ned's OK about it. If you don't think you know the guy, and let's face it, he was a bit of a mystery to us all, go and find out about him. Talk to the people who really knew him. You know who they are. Ned will help you. You've got time before the funeral. Just go and get on with it. It's no big deal."

"Then how can I refuse?"

"You can't."

Clarke hoped that he wouldn't live to regret this half-hearted acceptance. Catherine gave him a warm smile and then reached over to peck him on the cheek.

"Hang on, I've got something that might help you."

Catherine squeezed his hand before dashing out of the room to run upstairs. Clarke traced her path across the ceiling in the dull thumps of her footsteps, cursing himself for not saying 'no'.

The footsteps stopped. A drawer was opened. The footsteps reversed their path.

When he looked down, Clarke noticed Sinéad staring at him from the far side of the breakfast bar. It startled him. Self-conscious, Clarke raised his eyebrows in acknowledgement, wanting to know what was on her mind. She glanced away shyly.

"Look, take this with you," Catherine said, as she marched back into the kitchen and thrust a battered Filofax into Clarke's hands with a triumphant smile.

"Jake's?"

"Absolutely."

Clarke eyed the book, wondering what dark secrets lurked within its tatty pages.

"Thanks very much," he mumbled, still failing to enthuse. "I'll see what I can do."

9.

Wednesday, am. The morning after receiving the news and life was already resuming its normal pattern. Clarke was disturbed by his ability to act as if nothing out of the ordinary had happened. The alarm woke him at 7am as usual. Up and out of bed quickly, he fixed himself a breakfast of cereal and coffee – as usual – was in and out of the shower in five minutes flat – as usual – got to the studio by the same route and the same time – nine o'clock on the dot – as usual. It was raining – as usual.

However, once at his desk he didn't feel much like tackling any of the work log-jamming before him, even though he knew he would need to make a start on it at some point in the day, and deliver it the next, if he were going to make the funeral. To underline his plight the fax machine had spewed an avalanche of correspondence across the floor. He pushed the unwelcome pile of paperwork to one side to clear a space for the phone, his address book and Jake's Filofax.

It was fortunate that Catherine had set him a task to kick-start the day, as the temptation to just sit and feel sorry for himself loomed large. Somehow, he had to get his head around writing the address for Jake's funeral.

God, how much you forget! he thought. His first impressions of Jake? Well, you didn't need to know much about Jake to warm to him. Generous and affectionate, he offered instant friendship to anyone he met, hanging on to their every word – flirting a little, flattering a lot. Then again, there were times when he could turn cold and aloof – as much like a cat as a dog; at one moment in your face, delving into your personal life, wanting to know the most intimate details about your sex life, but then running for cover if you turned the conversation round to focus on his. He could be equally as open and honest as defensive and evasive. As equally at ease as uncomfortable and tense.

Clarke lifted the Filofax. Whilst he would prefer to improvise a speech off the top of his head, he knew he would have to do a bit of legwork first – sound out a few of Jake's friends – as Catherine had suggested. Being shy however, Clarke dreaded the thought. He hoped they wouldn't be like the couples he had met in Finchley earlier in the summer.

Black, battered and well-used, the Filofax bulged with menace. Clarke popped open the clasp. Inside the front cover small scraps of paper were crammed into a cellophane pocket. Clarke toyed with the idea of emptying them onto the desktop, but thought better of it. The pages of the telephone directory were smothered in scribbled phone numbers and fading addresses. Clarke was interested to see if Jake had any celebs stored among the riff-raff. Sure enough, he came across the odd writer, agent or publisher whose name he recognised, but nothing too flash. He checked to see if there was anyone he might have missed when phoning the day before. There were no names that stood out. Everybody would know by now anyway.

About to discard the book, curiosity got the better of him and he turned back to the plastic pocket at the front of the book. With the nimble fingers of a croupier, he extracted the mishmash of papers and shuffled them across the desk, face up. An absolute jumble, they were more like the contents of a wastepaper bin than a personal organiser: there were the fading remains of a book of postage stamps containing a couple of one-pence stamps – never coming in handy as once hoped; two under-exposed passport photographs of Jake looking very pale and emaciated, like an alien – *maybe he was an alien*; a photo – a happy scene – taken a good few years before, of Jake and his two kids on a beach, probably Donegal, the kids perched high on his shoulders; a rather poignant scrap of paper with the inscription *'To Jake, from Daddy, with love'* scrawled in pencil; a greetings card from the father of a former girlfriend thanking him for a book he had sent him and extolling Jake's virtues; a couple of Polaroids, one of Catherine McCullough with long strawberry-blonde hair and their first child, Thomas, in her arms; the other, a family group. It was a photo taken four or five years earlier – of Clarke, his wife and their two kids posing with plumes of candyfloss at a funfair; Old Deer Park, Richmond, he remembered. He turned the Polaroid over and moved on quickly, before becoming too melancholic. Next: the business card of a taxi rank in Finsbury; then the photo of some anonymous tot taking its first faltering steps; and an ageing and folded compliments slip from a publisher in London, which when unravelled revealed a message written in neat black biro:

Dear Jake,
How goes it? I've made a break from the PPL Publishing House. The change is not too dramatic – remember Michael Silverman? Well, I'm under his expert tutorship.
It's a small world in publishing! You should drop in and see us if you're in London Town...
All the best,
 Jane (Etherington).

Clarke stuffed the dilapidated ephemera back inside the cellophane sleeve, smiling, surprised that Jake had been carrying the little scraps of paper around with him like a bag lady, and that he had hung onto the photo of them taken at the fair.

Jake's hoard of sentimental curios reminded him of the last time he was in Grandfather Clarke's house, a 1930s semi in Northside,

Dublin. It was on the day of the old man's funeral. Clarke wanted to record the interior for posterity and take in its atmosphere one last time. To smell its smells. To memorise the fixtures and fittings. He took a camera. His uncle met him at the house, let him in and left him to it.

He stood in the hallway for the last time taking deep breaths, trying to capture the smell, the musty smell of old people, invoking memories of Boxing Days and Easter Sundays, bracing himself to let go.

In a way he wished that he hadn't brought the camera, but the temptation to keep a bit of his past, and the simplicity of doing it, was too strong. He didn't dwell long over the photography. A few minutes hurrying around and it was done. The atmosphere was all too pervasive, the objects too personal. There was something of the feel of Pompeii about the place, as though his grandfather had left the house just a few moments before. A pair of his glasses still sat unfolded on the kitchen table beside his pen and a bottle of life-preserving pills. He took the glasses and pen and left for the funeral, happy to escape the sentimentality.

Clarke blinked himself out of his daydream, refocusing his eyes on the Filofax in his hands.

The phone rang, waking him from the lethargy threatening the afternoon's work. He put the Filofax in a drawer and grabbed the telephone receiver before it tripped the answerphone.

"Hi, Charlie, it's Kay. I've just heard about Jake."

"Oh Jesus... Kay!"

Fuck, he thought. Why hadn't he phoned her?

"Shit! It's awful, Kay. I was about to phone you," he lied. "Who told you?"

"I heard it on the radio at lunchtime. It was on the news."

She sounded tired.

"Well yeah, I guess it would be. What did they say?"

"They didn't give much detail. They just said that he'd had a heart attack. Why? What else is there to know, Charlie?"

"Oh... Nothing really."

"How's Catherine?"

"She seems all right, but you know... The funeral's in Ireland, if you want to go."

"God, I can't afford that, Charlie."

"Look, I'm really sorry I didn't phone."

"No problem. You've got other priorities these days."

A touch of sarcasm had crept into her voice.

"Look, I'm going to get off the line, Kay, in case Catherine's trying to get through. I'll give you a call when I get back next week... OK?"

"That's fine, Charlie. You do that– "

She put the down phone abruptly.

"Bye Kay– " Clarke said belatedly, wondering whether he should have made a greater effort to talk to her.

He could have phoned her back, but didn't want to. Truth be told, he couldn't be bothered. He didn't have the mental energy to sustain a normal conversation with Kay now that she was his ex-wife. A normal conversation would have been a luxury, but they hadn't had a 'normal conversation' for an age. Talking to her on the phone just hurt. It brought back so much of the sadness. He knew that this reaction suggested that he still loved her – which he did. And he could tell that she still loved him by the way that she always sounded bitter and aggressive whenever they talked. And that was just it. That was why he would rather not phone her back.

Although the divorce had been traumatic, living seemed a little easier for Clarke in the aftermath. It was a happier life, not entirely happy, but one he could tolerate. It was gentler on him. That wasn't to say that there weren't occasional highs, but the vitality he had enjoyed with Kay when they were first married – when the children were born – was gone. Totally gone. He felt the current of his life had lost its energy, its flow. Now it meandered, a trickle.

Clarke sat staring into space, nursing his emotions and trying to distance himself from fonder memories of his ex-wife. Looking around his desk he decided to put off making any more calls until the next day. He'd had enough stress for the time being and needed to get on with some work.

Just about to turn on his Apple Mac, he noticed that the crumpled compliments slip from Jake's Filofax had dropped out onto the floor. He picked it up and studied the youthful hand. *Who the hell is Jane Etherington?* he wondered. Maybe he should call. He picked up the receiver and tapped in the digits before he could change his mind.

Why was he doing this? he asked himself. *For Jake, of course.* Yes, he was doing this for Jake. Jake would want a big turnout for his funeral, and that was what he had to ensure.

The phone was answered sooner than he had hoped.

"Stewart, Tench and Bell. Can I help you?" a voice chirped down the receiver.

"Oh yes. Hello... Is Jane there please?"

"Partridge or Pearson?"

"Etherington?"

"Left last month."

"Oh. Have you– "

"No sir, not allowed." The voice sounded sterner by the syllable. "Sorry. We can't give out personal numbers."

"Oh, that's a pity. Jane really needs to know. I'm phoning from the clinic. I've got the results of a test she took in August... Oh well, never mind."

Clarke was surprised by his cunning.

"What kind of test?"

"I'm afraid I can't give that information out over the phone... but it's a pity. She needs to know, and this is the only number she left us."

"Tudor Grove," the voice cut in.

"No, Osbourne Street."

"No sir, not your clinic... Tudor Grove, you know Tudor Grove? It's the name of the publishing company she works for now. Number's in the book," the voice said, amused to discover a telephone manner as flaky as her own.

Clarke didn't waste any time. As soon as the receiver was replaced he got the Tudor Grove number and hammered out the digits.

64

"Good morning, Tudor Grove Publishing."

"Jane Etherington please," Clarke said, bracing himself to go through his 'Jake's dead' announcement again.

"One moment please…"

The receptionist left him with an ear-splitting recording of *Winter* from Vivaldi's *Four Seasons* for company.

"Yep. Jane Etherington. How can I help you?" a voice barked into his ear.

"Hello, my name's Charlie Clarke. I'm a friend of Jake McCullough's."

"Oh, are you?"

"I was wondering if you knew?"

"Yes, I've heard, thanks very much. Anyway, who gave you my name and why are you phoning me?"

Clarke didn't know what was bugging her, but hoped it wasn't catching.

"I'm an old friend of Jake's. I've been phoning around to make sure everyone knows what's happened, and what the funeral arrangements are."

"And what are they?"

"We don't know yet," he said, using the 'we' to give himself authority.

"Well, I already know about Jake, and you don't know anything about the funeral arrangements, so why are you phoning me?"

"I'm sorry. It's just… well, to be perfectly honest, it's… it's something to do… I mean… something to keep my mind off the whole thing… Well, that's silly really… I mean, it just helps to keep busy– "

"Busy as in being a busybody, you mean?"

"Well look… if you must know, I didn't really know the guy that well… I mean I've known him for years – since I was seventeen in fact – but I didn't really get to know him… and… I kind of want to… I kind of need to as well… for a eulogy… and I just thought talking to people, to different people, might help."

"What do you expect me to do?"

"I was wondering if you would tell me what you know about Jake."

"Why?"

"Why not?"

"When?"

"Now?"

"I haven't got time, Mr... Sorry, what did you say your name was?"

"Clarke."

"Mr Clarke."

"Charlie..."

"Ah, yes. He mentioned you, actually," she said, assuming a more relaxed tone.

"OK. When?"

"Oh, I can't remember now."

"No, I mean when can you see me?"

"Where are you?"

"Battersea."

"Right. Do you know the Groucho Club?"

"In Dean Street... Yes."

"Are you a member?"

"No."

"I am. I'll meet you in there at 7.30 tonight. If you're there before me, give my name at the desk and they'll show you into the bar. We'll talk about Jake. And Mr Clarke... whatever you hear... you hear in confidence. All right?"

"Sure."

"And I must warn you, Mr Clarke. My bite is worse than my bark."

And with that she was gone. Clarke slumped back in his chair, blew his cheeks out, tilted his head back to search the ceiling for inspiration and thought... *Who the hell was that?*

10.

Charlie Clarke arrived in Soho with plenty of time for a couple of pints before his rendezvous with Jane Etherington. He wanted to be relaxed enough to cope with what he imagined would be a forceful personality. The prospect made him anxious. His life had become dominated by routine in the last couple of years and anything that didn't fit into his usual pattern was to be avoided. He had got out of the habit of meeting new people and wasn't sure why he was putting himself through this particular ordeal now. But he was curious about how this woman knew Jake. Jake had never mentioned her. And what had she meant when she said: '*whatever you hear, you hear in confidence*?' What did she have to hide?

A sudden frisson of excitement enlivened his senses, awakening a taste for adventure long dormant but which he now felt happy to indulge.

Before leaving home he had tried phoning Ned Labinski to see if there was any news from the coroner's office, and to quiz him about Jane Etherington. Ned wasn't at home or in Finchley, however, and his mobile was either switched off or had become another casualty of the damp weather.

Clarke wasn't enthusiastic about meeting at the Groucho Club. He'd been there a few times before, and although he liked the interior and found the staff pleasant, the thought of socialising in a watering hole packed with media types was too much for him to bear midweek. Two pints in the Dog and Duck on Frith Street helped warm him to the idea, however.

Clarke was the first to arrive at the Groucho. The bar was library quiet. He sank low into a battered sofa and hid behind the final edition of the *Evening Standard*, which he flicked through to look for any mention of Jake and, sure enough, found a report in the arts pages plus a brief obituary. The obituary didn't offer much more than a *Who's Who* entry:

Jake McCullough, the children's book author, best known for the popular cartoon character Johnny-One-Foot, the Footballing Penguin, has died following a sudden heart attack.

McCullough was the recipient of this year's Northern and West Building Society literary award for the Best New Writer in Children's Publishing.

McCullough's first three novels: 'The Pigeon Letters', 'Eye of the Beholder' and 'Laura's Pantry' were published in consecutive years between 1990 - 1993 by Daventry Press.

Born in Clove Rock, County Londonderry, Northern Ireland, McCullough is survived by a wife and two children.

Clarke cursed himself for not doing more and wished he had submitted a piece. He could write, for God's sake. Still, the obituary was a great ad for the Northern and West.

Looking up from the paper, he scanned the bar. The club was still entertaining the early evening crowd, bracing themselves for the journey home from work. The air was pretty smoky, but as an habitual ex-smoker – a one-or-two-a-week man – he liked it that way. He felt anonymous in the crowd and more comfortable than he had expected. Before long a small dark-haired woman marched into view, trailed by the front-of-house receptionist.

"Mr Clarke? Hello. I'm Jane Etherington," the small woman said, with a broad smile, fixing him with bright green eyes. "I'm sorry, but I've forgotten your first name."

She stretched out a tiny white hand for him to shake.

"It's Charles... Charlie," he said, levering himself out of his seat. She seemed to become more petite the further he rose up to greet her.

When they sat down she ordered a bottle of the house white and two glasses.

"Now, Charles, why are we here?"

"Jake McCullough."

"What about Jake?"

She was looking down on him from a firm leather armchair pulled up close to the low sofa on which he was sprawled.

"Jake was a dear friend. His wife has asked me to say a few words at the funeral. I haven't seen much of him over the last few years and want to find out what he's been up to. I just need to talk about him... I want to find out more about him... to talk to anyone who knew him better than I of late... I find that talking helps."

He felt ridiculous. His chair was so much lower than hers that he seemed to be talking to her knees, if not her knickers, which for someone over six feet tall was no mean feat.

He was drawn to her face, to her eyes – so very clear and bright. There was a hint of shyness in her expression that he hadn't anticipated on the phone. He was impressed with her manners.

"Mmm. I don't think I'm just *anyone*, Charles."

"But how do you know Jake?"

He was trying to prop himself up so he could at least be at her eye level.

"We met at work."

"Yeah?"

"Ooh, I'd say it was about eleven or twelve years ago. I was just out of university. He was a fair bit older than me. We were both working for a publishing company. It was quite near here actually. He was working in the design department, I think. I'm not sure. He might have moved on to copywriting by then... anyway... we were working together, and became great friends... How about you, Charles? How do you know him? From college?"

"I've known him since I was about seventeen. We've always been friends. I haven't seen that much of him in recent years, but we kept in touch. I'd been seeing a bit more of him of late. Well, thank God, really. I guess I was lucky in that respect. The last two or three times we had a really good laugh and got on well. I suppose at least I've got that to be thankful for."

"Yes, you're very lucky. I haven't spoken to him for a while."

"So?"

"So... We had some pretty wild adventures. More, once he'd left the company. We used to go out whenever he came up from Devon on business. We had some really good times. Yeah, pretty wild," she said, smiling again.

God, she was so very attractive, he thought. Jake must have gone for her in a big way. She was short, but with an hourglass figure, the kind men fall for big time. Everything about her was strong – formidable – her dark features, her bone structure, her eyes.

"And how 'close' were you and Jake?" Clarke asked, emboldened by drink.

"That's none of your business. He was married."

She poured them both another glass of wine before continuing.

"Anyhow, Charlie, if you're such a big friend of Jake's, how come I've never heard of you?"

"Come on. That's not true. You said you had earlier."

"He mentioned your name in passing, but that doesn't amount to much."

"Well, I could say the same. I'd never heard of you before today, and I'm surprised. It wouldn't be like him to keep someone as charming as you to himself."

"Oh piss off," she snapped playfully.

"Did you ever meet his wife?"

"No."

"Why not?"

"She was never around. I've spoken to her on the phone a couple of times, though. She sounds OK."

"She is."

"How is she doing?"

"She's very strong, but then you never know with something like this, do you?"

"And how about Ned?"

"Labinski?"

"Yes."

"You know him too?"

Clarke was surprised.

"Not very well. I've only met him once or twice. Jake talked about him all the time, though. So actually... in a way... I suppose I feel I know him quite well, if you know what I mean? I know he and Jake were close. How is he, anyway?"

"Oh, he seems fine right now, but then he's got a lot to do... a lot to organise. You know. He's kind of preoccupied for the moment."

"Anyway, how did you get my number, Charles?"

"It was on a compliments slip I found in Jake's Filofax."

"Oh. And what are you doing with Jake's Filofax?"

"Nothing. It's... it's... Oh never mind."

Clarke could sense that she wasn't really interested in the detail. He was surprised by Jane Etherington's cheek. He admired her directness.

"I must say, you're better looking than you sounded on the phone, Mr Clarke."

"What?"

"I thought you were going to be a bit of a wet blanket, but I can see that there's more to you than that."

"Jesus, you can be very patronising."

"Not unattractive really. Sensitive, but not unattractive... and Irish... Mmm, I like Irish men. Actually, you remind me of Jake. I bet you've got the same geriatric sense of humour... Have you?"

"You're making me feel like a prize bull."

"Well, let's not go over the top."

By now Clarke was glad to have been prised out of his midweek routine, and into the company of this eccentric woman. The adventure was beginning to bring its rewards. He was particularly enjoying the wine, as was she, and once they had finished the first bottle, they were both more than eager to order a second, and then a third.

The conversation grew more ragged and wide-ranging, as they weaned themselves off the subject of Jake. The more they drank, the stronger the attraction grew, the more they touched and laughed, the more they made eye contact, and by the time the third bottle was served Clarke had lost all inhibitions and found himself flirting outrageously.

By the time the third bottle had been drunk Jane Etherington had moved onto the sofa beside him. Soon they were locked in each other's arms, her legs draped over his lap, which in turn led to a little kissing – all of which went unnoticed by the two or three stragglers still propping up the bar at 2am, an hour after closing time.

They ordered a fourth bottle of the house white, were refused, and without bothering to settle the bill and before good sense could prevail, found themselves falling through the door of the club and into the back of a cab, which was promptly directed to Jane Etherington's flat. Clarke's research had begun.

11.

Albert Lewis had always looked younger than his years. Until he was twenty-five he was blessed with the palest complexion: soft and salmon pink, capped with a thick mop of strawberry-blond hair. This proved a curse in his mid-teens, when the baby face denied him service in the local pub – an age at which his peers were discovering alcohol as an effective aphrodisiac.

As he grew older, however, the advantages of a youthful appearance became apparent. He grew into his looks. In his forties the clear pale skin browned, whilst the full head of hair took five years off him, the redness fading to a subtler sandy colour. With advancing old age, and whilst others developed fatter waistlines and arthritic joints, Albert maintained his figure and his agility, and, for longer than most, his boyish good looks.

When Albert passed away it came as a surprise to all who knew him. If anybody could be expected to cheat death, then many would have put their money on Albert. At the time of his death, Albert was ninety-five years old – still slim, still agile. The end was sudden. Visiting the local clinic for an annual 'flu jab, he collapsed in the waiting room. Rushed to hospital, he was pronounced dead on arrival. Heart attack. The sense of loss for his surviving relatives and many friends and neighbours was great. Few had envisaged life without Albert.

At first there was much sadness. Everybody in Hove knew Albert Lewis, it seemed. Later his supporters celebrated the memory of a long life lived to the full. Albert had resided for so long in his peaceful suburban avenue in Hove that he was accepted as a member of the indigenous population. There were few in the area who knew his roots were in South Wales. He was from Swansea. There was still a hint in his voice – a slight lilt that gave him away – but in that part of South East England where accents are common, his was no more noticeable than the next.

But now Albert's voice was silent. It was Wednesday afternoon, and he lay motionless in the deepest of sleeps.

Albert Lewis' current condition prevented him from passing the time of day with the young man beside him, as he would have been accustomed to do had they been reclining at his barber's or on the beach in Torquay. The other man was also dead. They were both beyond casual chitchat.

The men would have got on well, though. Jake McCullough enjoyed the company of OAPs. He respected their values, their politeness, and liked to hear their stories – especially if they were about the war. Jake would have turned on the charm, and the two of them would have laughed long and loud, but not now.

They were both lying inert in the depths of the Brighton Royal Infirmary, prone to the probing of expert fingers and unaware of the shafts of sunlight beaming through the small mortuary window to gently radiate their skin.

They were stretched out on their backs under flimsy polycotton sheets pulled high up over their heads to conceal their faces. At the other end bare feet poked out from under the covers, semi-erect and stiff. Each had a label tied with postal string to the big toe of their left foot, identifying them by name and number. They rested on hospital trolleys, having been removed that morning from the grid of twenty vaults along the far wall of the mortuary, where they had been stored like butchered meat for the last couple of days (except for Jake's short excursion for a post-mortem). Albert would have found it chilly in the mortuary.

They were both awaiting collection by the funeral firms appointed by their respective families.

Although it is not common, it is not unheard of for hospitals to mix up babies in a maternity ward. It has happened, and with very distressing consequences for the families involved. It is also not unheard of for hospitals to remove perfectly healthy organs or even a healthy limb during an operation. Accidents are common. Hospitals would not exist otherwise.

However, it has never been reported – though this doesn't mean to say that it has never happened – that a hospital has mixed up two corpses. But when Greystone and Sons Funeral Services came to collect Albert Lewis to take him home to Hove, and the elderly partner in the firm, Mr Greystone Senior, was left alone in the hospital mortuary without his reading glasses whilst the two mortuary attendants were called away to a union meeting – the odds of a mix-up shortened.

It was unfortunate therefore, when Jake McCullough was consigned to a Humanist cremation in nearby Hove whilst Albert Lewis was dispatched on his first overseas trip since D-day, to take a starring role in an Irish Catholic funeral in Northern Ireland; since McMullen and Co Funeral Directors of Finchley didn't think it necessary to check the label on Jake's foot, as there appeared to be only one body left out for collection.

Their fates were sealed.

12.

Charlie Clarke was aware of his hangover even before he awoke. It announced its arrival with a pounding cranial fanfare at five o'clock in the morning, demanding he get out of bed and quench the accompanying thirst with a gallon of water and a handful of tablets. Clarke ignored the directive, deciding that more sleep was of paramount importance – and then the alarm went off.

It was thinking about the alarm and its unfamiliar ring that reminded him he was not at home, but in a strange bed with company. This in turn prompted an immediate replay, video-style, of what he could remember of his night of passion with Jane Etherington – the two of them abandoning all clothing and scruples on the way from the front door to the bedroom of the petite studio flat. The picture paused at the moment she pulled off her bra as she bore down on him. Gorgeous breasts, he remembered from his bed's-eye view.

He blinked to wipe the memory and concentrate on the day ahead, struggling to arouse the work ethic. Time-conscious, he would normally be driven by a compulsion to get up and get going by now. There was too much work to finish with the funeral looming, to be fooling around with Jane Etherington. But thankfully his hangover was potent enough to take the edge off reality; so at that moment he couldn't care less.

Clapham looked wet and cold through the window. It was so warm and cosy in the bed, her bed. And there she lay, naked and hot and round. Graphic memories of the night before, combined with the persistent nagging of an early morning erection, encouraged him to stick out a hand to search for her body, her belly, her tenderest parts, to see if she might be as awake to the idea of a little early morning sex as he was.

His fingers were successful in their search and with a little gentle foreplay he found Jane Etherington, still groggy with sleep, as responsive as he was keen.

Sod work! he thought in uncharacteristic fashion.

The next time Clarke woke up he was relieved to find that the hangover hadn't matured into quite the force threatened earlier in the morning. He also realised he was alone in the bed.

"Would you like a coffee?" a voice shouted from downstairs.

"White, no sugar please," Clarke called back, finding it difficult to manipulate his mouth. He tried to analyse her tone. It sounded friendly enough.

Is this a good idea? was the next anxious thought to breach the hangover. That, and an irritating sense of guilt. He could never understand why he always felt guilty the morning after sex. Or was it claustrophobia?

Is this a good idea? he asked himself again.

Of course, he replied decisively. Why should he have any regrets? But then her words came ringing back over and over in his head: *'My bite is worse than my bark... My bite is worse than my bark.'*

Clarke shook his head and encouraged himself to go with the flow, but couldn't help thinking about Jake, and couldn't help wondering about Jake and Jane. What the hell had their relationship been? And then he couldn't help thinking about Jake, Jane and Catherine. *Jesus*, he didn't want to make life any more awkward for Catherine.

Jane Etherington came back into the room with coffee and toast and a broad smile. He was relieved that she still appeared as attractive to him in the cold light of day as she had the night before.

"I shouldn't be here you know, you bastard," she said, glancing at her watch.

"That makes two of us. I'm flying to Ireland in a couple of days' time, and I've got stacks to do."

"I wish I could go, but I've got a conference. It would be hard to get out of. Actually, if I *could* afford the time, I couldn't afford the ticket. I hate funerals, anyway."

This seemed strange to Clarke. Northern Ireland was a short hop by plane – it wouldn't be that expensive. Surely she would want to attend the funeral if she and Jake were such great mates. Surely her employer would give her time off for a funeral, conference or no. He wondered if her reluctance had anything to do with the prospect of meeting Catherine.

Clarke was relieved that she wouldn't be going, however. It would be a complication he could do without. If they went as a 'couple' it would create a sideshow, and although the idea of a romantic weekend away in Ireland had its appeal, he wouldn't try to talk her into it. She would only tell him to 'fuck off' if he did.

"Hey, what about you and Jake, anyway?" Clarke asked – wishing that he hadn't as soon as the words left his mouth.

"Ask Ned," she replied. "I'm sure *he* can tell you everything you want to know."

Clarke was in a daze when he left the flat. A combination of fresh air, the drinking, the sex, Jane Etherington and the intriguing question of her relationship with Jake. It wasn't that Clarke cared about what she had or hadn't done with Jake, it was just that in the short time since Catherine had asked him to take care of the eulogy and do some research, he hadn't expected to uncover anything contentious.

If his hunch about Jake and Jane Etherington was correct, and it seemed pretty obvious that they were more than friends, then he wasn't sure if he felt comfortable with the profile of Jake McCullough that was emerging. If he'd had one affair, he might well have had others. Jake had always been carefree – he was definitely the type.

It would soon be lunchtime and Clarke was keen to get to the studio and get on with some work; he also wanted confirmation from Ned or Catherine about the funeral arrangements. As soon as he arrived he phoned around looking for Ned. He found him at Catherine's. He was going to stay with her until after the funeral.

"What? How the hell did you find her?"

Clarke couldn't tell whether Ned was shocked or angry.

"Catherine gave me Jake's Filofax."

"Did she, now. Oh well, I'm sure you don't need me to tell you that you can take a lot of what Jane Etherington has to say with a pinch of salt."

"Yeah, maybe," Clarke mumbled. "What about the funeral?" he continued.

"I phoned the coroner's office this morning. Off the record, he said the post-mortem will show that Jake died of natural causes. Whatever the circumstantial evidence, there's no proof to the contrary. Without proof they can't record it as a suicide, thank God."

"So what happens next?"

"The coroner's going to release the body tomorrow when we get the death certificate. Then Jake'll be transported to Stranraer by the undertakers here, and met off the ferry in Belfast by the local firm from South Derry."

"So when's the funeral?"

"I guess if he arrives back in Derry on Friday or Saturday, it'll be this weekend."

"Yeah, that figures... That'll leave time enough for the wake, the open coffin and all that jazz. His family won't let Catherine get out of that one. Anyway, how is Catherine?"

"Not bad. Sinéad's with her."

"And you?'

"Oh, I'm fine."

"Jane Etherington says you can tell me all there is to know about her and Jake."

"Jesus Christ, Charlie! There's *nothing* to know."

"Fine, fine. I'm probably better off not knowing."

"Anyway, how did you two get on?"

"None of your business," Clarke said putting the phone down. He too could be evasive.

Once he had got rid of Ned, Clarke had a telephone blitz to unburden himself of any outstanding responsibility to those relying on him for news. He wanted the job over with as soon as possible. The last call made, he breathed a long sigh of relief.

Of the twenty people he had been in touch with since Jake's death, about half thought they could attend the funeral – the rest either had family or work commitments or implied that they couldn't afford the trip. Jake would have hoped for a better turnout.

Clarke booked his flight for the Saturday and coordinated with Ned with regard to accommodation. They would both stay at Jake's mother's house in Clove Rock. They would arrive on the Saturday night, leaving plenty of time to catch up on the Sunday morning before the funeral on the Monday.

Clarke called Jane Etherington again.

After giving him some abuse for making her late for work, her mood grew more friendly. It was quite a culture shock. He wasn't sure which made him more nervous, the friendly persona or the rude one. Rudeness seemed more honest.

To his relief, she confirmed that she wouldn't be going at the weekend. Then the conversation dragged. She intimated that she was busy and didn't have long to talk. Beads of sweat formed on his brow. He wanted to ask her out to dinner, for a drink, anything to keep things going, but was too frightened to make a move and unsure if he should, bearing in mind his reservations about her and Jake. As the conversation drew to a conclusion, he felt like a rabbit caught in headlights. Finally, and just before she hung up, he asked if she had any spare time to see him before he left for Ireland. She offered to meet him for a lunchtime drink on the Friday.

It would be interesting to meet her sober, he thought. The rush of adrenalin that followed the call could only be stemmed by rapidly smoking the battered cigarette he found at the back of the bottom drawer. Clarke inhaled deep lungfuls whilst staring into the bright daylight beyond the studio window, wallowing in the nicotine rush and mesmerised by the rolling plumes of cigarette smoke.

Before it burnt his fingers, Clarke stubbed out the butt and recovered his bearings. Thank God he'd got shot of the phone calls, he thought. But the telephoning had been therapeutic in helping to dissipate the grief. He had also gathered some useful information for his address. *Jesus...* the bloody eulogy. He had forgotten all about it.

Clarke had never felt less confident. It wasn't that he had a fear of public speaking – he was more than competent – but confident about Jake's eulogy? Not at all.

Since Clarke came from an Irish family, he was no stranger to the requiem mass and had sat through many eulogies. He knew what was expected and would have no trouble in writing the appropriate words. But he wanted to be sincere. He didn't want to serve up sentimental claptrap. Jake had obviously made mistakes, but the mistakes were as much a legacy as his successes.

Then there was the pressure of Jake's close family and friends, who thought the man a saint. They wouldn't want their illusions shattered. Clarke sighed a troubled sigh and attempted to lose himself in work.

13.

Charlie Clarke dropped by to see Jake's mother on his way home from the studio. As Breige McCullough had known him since he was a teenager, he was confident of a warm reception and hoped she would feel relaxed enough to talk about Jake. Nevertheless he knew it wouldn't be an easy meeting. Clarke walked slowly.

Breige was staying at Orla's flat in Battersea. Orla lived close by Clarke's apartment on Battersea Park Road, but at the opposite end. The road ran the length of the park from Battersea Bridge in the east to Chelsea Bridge in the west, and although she was only about three quarters of a mile away, he had never visited her, and couldn't remember bumping into her on the street either.

Clarke rang the doorbell, half hoping that mother and daughter would be out. It seemed to take forever for anyone to come to the door.

"*Hello?*" a voice croaked through the intercom.

It was a frail voice which made only a vague connection with his memory of Breige McCullough.

"It's Charlie... Charlie Clarke, Breige."

He pronounced each syllable with the careful emphasis and added volume of a shopkeeper serving a foreign tourist.

"*Push the door and come up,*" the voice crackled from the intercom.

The lobby and stairs smelt musty – the aroma of damp rot in full bloom. The carpet was of a hard-wearing grey synthetic material that threatened static and boasted the black scuff-marks of a busy life. The walls, once cream, bore a brown hue, etched by hundreds of passing hands. It concerned Clarke that Breige was staying in such squalid surroundings and he wondered if Jake had known how run-down Orla's mansion flat had become.

"Hiya, Breige. How are you keeping?" Clarke beamed, as she met him at the top of the stairs. He clasped her hands and tried to appear buoyant.

"Oh, Charlie... why did he do it? Did you have any idea he was going to do that... did you?" Breige asked, running roughshod over the niceties of greeting and unsettling him immediately.

"No... No I didn't..," he stammered, taken aback by her directness. It was so much easier to say 'no' to shut her up. "But, Breige, you don't really think he did it, do you? It was a heart attack, after all."

Breige ignored him and led him into the sitting room. It was a relief to find that the interior of the flat was much smarter than the lobby. The rooms were spacious and well proportioned, offering good views across Battersea Park towards Albert Bridge and the Thames.

"I'm sorry about the mess. Orla's rather casual like that, and I just haven't had the energy for housework."

"Oh, it's fine Breige... Anyway, where is she?"

"She's gone up to Finchley."

"Oh... right."

"Look, Charlie, I know my son damn well. He was far too young to have had a coronary," Breige said, sticking to her theme. "You know how he liked to drink. He poisoned himself, Charlie. I'm sure of it. It's as simple as that."

"How can you be sure, Breige?" Clarke said, trying to fudge the issue.

"Haven't you heard how they found him? It was all the hotel could do to keep the newspapers out of it... but that won't last. Apparently, the hotel room was brimming with drink, Charlie. Bottles and bottles of the stuff. The staff could hardly get the door open to get him out. Why would a hotel resident have four cases of vodka in their room, for God's sake? He wasn't selling it," she said with a curious cackle that led to a cough. "I haven't said anything to Catherine. I wouldn't. But I know."

"So why did the coroner say it was death by natural causes?"

"Because of the alcohol. Because he had been at a rowdy party. Because he didn't leave a note. Because there was no apparent reason. Maybe because he's Irish and they think this is normal behaviour where we're from... I just don't know."

"Are you sure it wasn't an accident, Breige?"

"Oh yes. I'm very sure. He was practically an alcoholic, Charlie. He wouldn't have done it by mistake."

She sat shaking her head.

"But are you really sure, Breige?"

"Look, Charlie, he's always had addictive tendencies. He didn't think I noticed. What a fool... Just because I'm his mother he thinks I don't have eyes... or ears. I used to phone him in the evening, but he was always drunk. He tried to hide it, but I could hear it in his voice – I could almost smell it. So then I used to phone him in the mornings, but then he could barely speak because of the hangovers. His voice would be low and coarse – he would blame it on a cold. A cold! He had that cold for two years. So then I would call him in the afternoon. About two o'clock in the afternoon. Well, I had to stop. He would be drunk then, too. Again, he'd try and hide it, but I could still hear it in his voice. God knows how Catherine coped. Well... God and me."

"What?"

"Well, let's just say I know; I know how she coped. The same way I coped with his father. He was just the same. He could be quite abusive, too. The abuse was never physical, Charlie, and I mean... never. But the verbal abuse. My God, the things he would say to me. Cope? You don't cope. You just wait. You just wait for it to pass. Again and again. Charlie, have you noticed how composed Catherine has been? And why is that, do you think? I'll tell you why: because she is relieved. Yes. She is bloody relieved. For the first time since God knows when, she doesn't have to live in fear.

She hasn't had to wait around wondering when it's going to start all over again... all the verbal abuse. The shouting, the crying."

"Are you sure, Breige?"

"No, I'm not sure. I could be completely wrong. But I *know*. I can sense it. I've experienced it. And I'm his mother."

"Look, Breige, what you're saying could be... probably is, all true... but he was a fantastic man. He had many saving graces."

"Yes of course. But God, he had ridiculously high standards for himself and he just couldn't meet them. He'd always been ambitious, ever since school. He was a brilliant writer. A brilliant writer. Did you read any of his books, Charlie?"

"Yeah, the first two or three."

"But *he* didn't think he was any good, you see. He considered that he was just about mediocre. The trouble was his novels weren't very commercial. They were very personal. Probably too personal. And he wouldn't compromise. He refused, but at the same time he was too hard on himself. I think it affected his confidence in the last two or three years."

"So what about Johnny?"

"Johnny-One-Foot?"

"He's made a packet out of that penguin over the years."

"Look, Charlie, Jake hated Johnny... Actually he blamed him... He wanted recognition for his serious work and didn't get it. You see, he feared mediocrity. He loathed the very thought of it. He thought poor Johnny was a little bit of a lightweight. Johnny just made the situation worse. He didn't want the money, he just wanted respect. I mean, he tried everything. Even before the writing he'd tried drawing, painting, sculpture, journalism and teaching. He really thought he had found something when he began to write. He loved it at first. The freedom to express himself, and all that... the creativity.

"People liked what he wrote, too, Charlie, and he was very optimistic. But the initial euphoria ended and he wasn't getting the recognition he craved. Then Johnny-One-Foot took off... At first he thought it hilarious, but the joke didn't last long. It just looked as though he was only going to be 'mediocre' as a writer too, just as he had been at everything else. Of course, what the fool didn't realise was that his great talent was for living. For being himself. Everybody loved Jake, Charlie– ”

“Yeah. Absolutely, Breige.”

“Everybody. Complete strangers. He was so harmless, and absolutely loveable. But then his demons caught up with him. You know... his ambition. I guess he was greedy in a way, but he had such a big vision, Charlie. He wanted so much from life, but believed himself so average. That's probably when he took to drink.”

“And you're sure about this?”

“Damn sure. Have you seen how calm the children are? Don't you wonder why? For the first time in ages they feel relaxed... relaxed because they've stopped living in fear... Charlie, I *am* damn sure... I saw it happen to his father. That's why I blame myself. I should have been able to do something this time. But you see, Charlie, like his father... he was so damn stubborn.”

“Yeah, I know. I'm sorry too. I was his friend. I always thought he was happy. He always seemed so in control. But they're the ones that you least suspect... the smiling ones.”

Clarke paused.

“Maybe he wore his smile like a raincoat... like, when the clouds came... He'd told me that Catherine had been complaining about his drinking, but I dismissed it. We actually laughed about it. I guess I could have done more to help him.”

Clarke shrugged.

“We all could have done more, Charlie, but I guess ultimately he would have turned us away. He could be very pig-headed.”

Breige started to stand up. It was obvious that his time was up.

“Well, are you coming home for the funeral, Charlie? I'm sure I don't have to ask.”

Breige reached for Clarke's hand when she noticed tears gathering in his eyes.

“Yeah. Of course. There'll be a few coming over from here.”

“Good. He would like a big crowd.”

14.

A big crowd is exactly what greeted Jake McCullough as the hearse dawdled towards the crematorium on the Hove ring road. Heads were bowed and expressions solemn. Children were kept from running on the grass verges, and those prone to fits of the giggles were carefully marshalled by their parents. Due reverence was shown towards the coffin as it edged through the large crowd waiting outside the chapel of rest for Albert Lewis. The chapel, a concrete bunker flattered by well-kept gardens, gleamed in the flashes of sunshine breaking through the cloud cover.

If his ears could hear, Jake would have known he was at the wrong funeral the moment the opening bars of Louis Armstrong's *What a Wonderful World* played on the chapel's tinny sound system as he was carried up the aisle. Albert's musical taste was for easy listening: MOR.

Jake had sometimes wondered what it would be like to attend his own funeral – to sit at the back of the chapel and see who would turn up, who of his friends would be emotional and who would be unmoved. Now, however, he would not be attending dead or alive.

There was barely enough room at Albert's funeral service to squeeze all the mourners into the chapel, either standing up or sitting down. Latecomers had to listen to the proceedings from outside, straining to hear through cupped hands pressed tight to the cold wooden doors. Albert Lewis was an institution in Hove.

None at the chapel would have been aware that Albert's remains were many miles away, soon to embark on the brief sea crossing from Stranraer to Belfast, and none could have been aware of the discomfort that the occupant of Albert's coffin would have suffered, had he known that the lid of the maple box was decked out in the Union flag, Albert's wartime service medals, and the battered, but much-loved, Panama he wore when playing bowls.

The order of service would have brought Jake some succour, however, for Albert was an atheist. The ad hoc service chosen for the aged bachelor by his adoring nieces and nephews was conducted by a Humanist specialising in non-Christian funeral rites. The readings had no religious context. Rather than the psalms or gospels, the texts came from the writings of Native American Indians and the war poets. There were no hymns, but tapes of Albert's favourite songs – an eclectic mix of hits such as *Roll Along Covered Wagon* by Harry Roy and his orchestra and Lee Marvin's gravelly rendition of *Wand'rin' Star* from *Paint Your Wagon*. Many tears were shed.

Meanwhile Albert was missing his big day on the A76 in Scotland, somewhere along the Solway Firth between Dumfries and Stranraer.

In due course Jake's ashes were presented to Albert's grieving relatives – some of whom were for keeping them as a memento, preserving them, as if they still possessed a life-force. Initially the ashes – which had been placed in a gleaming silver urn – rested on the mantelpiece in the home of his eldest niece, Kathleen, where the core of the funeral service gathered for a drink and a sandwich.

After a lengthy debate, good sense prevailed and it was agreed that the ashes would be spread in the goalmouth at the Goldstone Road end of Albert's much-beloved Brighton and Hove Albion Football Club. His spirit would will the team on in seasons to come. Later in the day a close-knit group of about a dozen of Albert's relatives assembled outside the ground – some needing the additional support of a shoulder or wall as a consequence of Kathleen's generous hospitality.

The party made its way to the chosen end of the pitch to gather under the goalposts, as arranged with the head groundsman, who, wary of the visitors, monitored their progress through binoculars in the main stand.

The stadium had a ghost-town greyness without its regular Saturday afternoon crowd. It was also well-worn and scruffy, having seen more prosperous times – days when the team had played in the higher divisions of the football league. On the pitch a light drizzle kept spirits dampened. Shivering beneath the goalposts, Kathleen, who was carrying Albert's urn (and therefore Jake's ashes), looked up at the others in the group, waiting for instruction. None came.

No one was sure how to conduct the spreading of the ashes. They felt a need for ritual, for someone to seize the initiative and give the affair some kind of form, but no one volunteered. There was an awkward silence whilst they waited for inspiration. None came. There was no protocol for them to follow except that which they could concoct from a diet of television soap opera, situation comedy and American film.

Kathleen took control.

"I am going to sprinkle Albert's ashes. Does anyone want to say a few words? Does anyone want to say a prayer or anything?"

No one stirred.

"Right then. Here goes."

Kathleen removed the lid with stern concentration, passing it to her teenage son with care, her grip on the polished silverware challenged by woollen mittens.

"Rest in peace, Albert. We love you, miss you, and will think of you always... with fondness..."

And with that Kathleen Stubbs, née Lewis, shook Jake's remains around the goalmouth as best she could, and as if she were spreading chicken feed. She was startled when three dusty cigarette stubs popped out among the ashes – appalled to think that anyone could have used Albert's urn as an ash tray. The wind got up and disturbed the regular pattern that Kathleen was attempting to create along the goal-line, which looked uncannily like a giant line of coke. The ashes drifted downfield towards the centre circle. This was not the desired effect. But no matter.

In the stand the groundsman tutted. He knew the nature of the wind and how it could swirl around the ground. He lifted his binoculars and focused the lenses on the small group in the goalmouth in anticipation of the next gust. It soon arrived, whipping at Kathleen's neat pile, which was hurled into the air above the mourner's heads and then commenced to fall on them in a fine powder. Framed in the bowl of the groundsman's glasses, they looked like characters in a snow globe.

Flecks of ash gently settled on the shoulders, shoes and trouser bottoms of Albert's family, causing much embarrassed arm-flapping and trouser-brushing. Evidently, some of them would be carrying home rather more than fond memories of Albert Lewis.

After a few moments of contemplation, they left the grey-brown stain lying along the goal-line and withdrew in silence towards the exit, the job done. As the party progressed through to the back of the main stand the wind gusted again, blowing across what was left of the ashen pile and tossing the larger flakes high into the air and then over the stadium roof. The wind then continued to blow Jake's remains to the south east, out to sea and still further away from Ireland in the west.

15.

Friday morning, and for once Charlie Clarke woke up in his own bed, alone, and without a hangover. He was glad it was Friday, the last day at work before packing up for the weekend trip to Ireland. Fridays always felt a little like the end of term.

When he got to work, Clarke was relieved to find that there were no messages on the answerphone. Thank God; he didn't have another phone call in him. His ability to be compassionate was wearing thin.

Getting down to work he busied himself with finishing the priority jobs and then organised his daybook to make sure that he wouldn't forget any previously arranged work commitments on his return. At lunchtime he got a cab over to West Kensington to meet Jane Etherington. He had booked a table in a small trattoria off Kensington Church Street.

Clarke arrived first – a tactical ploy. As usual he wanted to allow for a large gin and tonic ahead of his date. The restaurant, a modest Italian, was empty. There was little to preoccupy him. While he waited, his imagination teased him with lurid images of Jake with Jane Etherington, and even though he guessed the reality would be tamer, he couldn't help but picture the most pornographic of scenarios. He wondered if she wouldn't find *him* dull in comparison to Jake.

Then she came into view, striding along the pavement: black hair and black trouser suit, a whirlwind of chutzpah, fierce green eyes and a smile that flashed white through fiery-red lipstick, oblivious to the rain.

"Hello, Charlie. Sorry to have kept you."

She leant forward to give him a kiss, warm and delicious.

"No problem, but I'm afraid I haven't got long."

"No need to apologise. You do that too often," she said, putting him further on the defensive. "Any news?"

"Not really. I saw Jake's mother last night– "

"And how was she?"

"OK... but I think she's got a long way to go. I think she blames herself a bit."

"Mmm... I wouldn't know," Jane Etherington mumbled dismissively as she tore open a bread roll. "Have you spoken to Ned yet?"

"Not really. He's too preoccupied with looking after Catherine and getting Jake back home to Ireland to be bothered with tittle-tattle right now. I'll get to talk to him better on Saturday."

"I think you'll be surprised," Jane Etherington teased.

"Mmm... I'm sure you're right."

They sat for a while, fiddling with the menu.

"You're a bit of a mystery yourself," she pronounced. "Tell me more..."

"There's not much to know."

"Parents?"

"Dead."

"Brothers and sisters?"

"One older sister."

"Wife?"

The question took Clarke by surprise. It made him realise how little they knew about each other.

He paused before answering.

"Can you tell?"

"What?"

"That I was married?"

"*Was* married?"

"Yeah... *was* married."

"Of course. You have the hangdog expression and world-weariness of a divorced man. A bit little-boy-lost. It's quite attractive really."

"Yeah, it wasn't a great experience, if you must know. It wasn't one of my great successes."

"What happened?"

"I have to say, Jane, for someone who'll tell me nothing, you are incredibly nosy."

"Oh, just tell me."

"It's not a very happy story. You've probably heard it before anyway. It gave me some... a lot of... unwanted publicity at the time."

"Oh, tell me anyway," she said, not taking him at all seriously. But then she stopped abruptly, caught her breath and looked into his eyes.

"Oh, Charlie... hang on a minute... You're the one, aren't you? It's you... I'm so sorry... You know I said that Jake had mentioned you a couple of times... Well, you're the one, aren't you? God, I can be so stupid– "

"Yeah, it was me."

"Oh Jesus, Charlie, I'm so sorry."

She searched for his hand.

"It's OK. It doesn't get any easier, you know."

"Look, you don't have to talk about it."

Clarke gazed into his glass looking for inspiration; gathering words and phrases with which to put together an honest re-telling of the story. He wanted to be precise. He rarely spoke of the matter now, but would make an exception for her. Bracing himself with a big swig of gin and tonic, Clarke launched right in.

"It was the weekend. It was Sunday morning. We'd all ripped the arse out of Friday and Saturday. Friday we'd gone round to the neighbours and drunk ourselves stupid. Saturday we rolled out of bed and got down to the pub for lunch as soon as we were physically able. By Sunday we were all in recovery. Sunday morning was pretty surreal anyway, thanks to the drink the day before and the weather, which was deliciously warm and dry for April. I was lying in the bath. It was so relaxing. I could have stayed there for hours... days... months..."

Clarke frowned as he heard himself slipping into the familiar monologue, repeating the well-rehearsed explanation. He continued, concentrating hard and speaking in a lowered voice. It was the only way he knew how to do it. "I was reading the *Sunday Times* sports section and listening to Classic FM on the radio. It was about ten o'clock. I'd just had breakfast with Kay and the kids. The kids were playing downstairs, they'd been pretty boisterous that morning. They'd been in the house for most of the weekend and had energy to burn. So I lay there in the bath, nursing my hangover. The water, just right... nice and hot. The music on the radio was soothing. Yeah, Albinoni, I think. Well, I know it was... the Albinoni... the *Adagio*... Anyway I was wallowing in my comfort zone and thinking: *Jesus, isn't this just the business?* when I suddenly hear the kids... shouting, mucking about and carrying on... playing a game of something or other. And I'm thinking, *God, look at what you've got*, and I lie there, counting my blessings... and I laugh to myself imagining their games downstairs and the *craic* they're probably having. Then I hear this scream. Oh God, I hear this scream..."

Clarke was whispering now, and tightening his fingers into fists.

"Look, Charlie, you don't have to tell me this, you know. You don't have to go through it all again for me," Jane Etherington said, gathering his knotted fists into her hands.

Clarke glanced up at her.

"It's OK. I don't mind telling you, if you don't mind listening."

"No, of course not. No... go on if it helps."

"Well, you see, I heard a scream. It was Kay's voice. It was very shrill, and very long, and very strange... I mean, I couldn't hear it that clearly over the sound of the radio, but I could hear it, and I knew immediately that something was wrong. Very wrong. It's a bit like when your kids are babies. You can soon learn the difference between their cries. You know... which cries are just for attention, which ones mean they're hungry, and those very telling cries when they are in pain... like when they've got an ear infection or something. I could tell this scream was a scream for help. My first thought was that the kids had hurt themselves. Anyway, I fling the paper to one side, leap out of the bath, and hurtle down the stairs. All the while Kay is screaming. And then I rush into the sitting room, where the noise is coming from, and then I see it... the blood... God, the blood."

Clarke stopped talking, trying to keep the tears at bay with silence, but he had to keep talking, and as he tried to utter the next few words, tears streamed down his face preventing him from saying any more. He broke down, his shoulders heaving like pistons.

"Oh God, Charlie– "

"No. I want to finish," he said, holding back the waves of emotion. "You see, I rush into the room and there's this kid. Jesus – barely a teenager, and he's holding a baseball bat, and he's wild, an animal, and he's trying to hit my wife with it, and she's trying to fend him off with her hands, with her bare hands, with her fingers. Fine dainty little fingers. And this bastard is trying to hit her with this bloody big baseball bat. And then he sees me, standing stark naked in the doorway, dripping wet... And he freezes... staring at me – blood splashed all over his face, his arms, his fucking smiley face T-shirt, his combat trousers, his trainers, the carpet, the walls. And my children are lying limp on the floor covered in blood. And he's staring into my eyes. And I can see no expression – nothing. Not a fucking thing... No fear, no evil, no wild rage... just nothing. And then he backs off and backs off and backs off. And it's over. The house is silent, except for Kay is sobbing. And for some weird reason I need Kay to be normal. Like I need her to say, 'Oh, never mind, darling, we'll soon sort this mess out' and we can't sort it out. And I'm just thinking, 'I know we can fix this... I'm sure we can fix this...' And of course, we can't.

And you know the thing that I can never forget for a second? The thing that haunts me..? The kids' voices. The kids' voices when I was sitting in the bath. Their screaming – screaming for help, while the bastard is beating them to death, and I think it's the sound of them playing and I'm lying there reading the paper and thinking how wonderful the world is."

"They caught the guy, right?"

"Yeah. He was fifteen. A bloody addict. High as a kite. Didn't know what he was doing... just looking to steal some cash to buy a fix. What a waste. And actually, Jane, I thought for a while recently that it was getting better, that I was getting over it, but it doesn't get any easier and you don't."

They sat in silence holding hands.

"Are you OK?" she asked after a while.

"I try to be. God, I try so hard to be OK. But it's the guilt that eats away at you. It destroyed my relationship with Kay. We never stood a chance after that day. We were both a permanent reminder to each other of what we had had, and what we had lost. We blamed each other. There was no blame, but we couldn't go on. It was just too much for us both to handle. And why do I feel guilty? I feel guilty for being so careless. Obviously, it wasn't my fault, but then again, maybe just in some small way I caused it. Maybe if I hadn't been so complacent. Oh, you know... but it's all so fucking confusing."

"Poor Charlie."

"I feel more sorry for my wife, actually. I'm not sure if she's as strong as me."

"Look, Charlie, maybe this isn't a good time to talk. Come round and have some dinner when you get back from Ireland. We'll talk then, if you want to."

They finished their meal in silence. The story left a void that idle chat wouldn't fill. As they left the restaurant, Clarke turned to Jane to say goodbye.

"You know I'm supposed to be gathering material for this damn eulogy... you know... talking to people who knew him recently?"

"Well?"

"Well, I haven't really got much further than you so far."

"Why are you so worried about it? It's not that important. Anyway, what do you expect to find out?"

"What do you mean?"

"Well, you're not Joseph Cotten."

"Who?"

"Joseph Cotten... He played the reporter in *Citizen Kane.*"

"What?"

"That's what I mean... this isn't *Citizen Kane.*"

"What?"

"You know, the film, *Citizen Kane*... Charles Foster Kane... Richest man in America... His dying words... well *word*... is 'Rosebud'," Jane Etherington said, affecting a deep and hoarse voice as though she too were dying. "The newspapers go mad trying to find out who Rosebud is... The reporter follows the trail of Kane's life talking to everybody who knew him... as he finds out about him so do we... blah, blah, blah."

"Yeah right," Clarke said, offhandedly. "And?"

"And what?"

"Who was Rosebud?"

"I don't know. Oh yeah... Not a 'who', a 'what'... an 'it'... It was a sledge. Yeah. The sledge he played with as a kid... When he was happy... Before coming into money and being sent away from his home to boarding school."

"Yeah, I remember. I saw it years ago."

"Well, listen... You're not Joseph Cotten, and you don't need to know everything there is to know about Jake McCullough."

"Maybe. Anyway, you haven't told me very much... Did *he* have a Rosebud?"

"Ask Ned. He'll know," she said, squeezing his arm and giving him an affectionate kiss.

They shared a brief hug outside the restaurant before going their separate ways.

"Look, Jane, I'll see you when I get back next week."

As he trudged off to the tube through the drizzle, he wondered if it hadn't been a little excessive to burden her with his past. Mind you, he consoled himself, she had asked the question.

Clarke phoned Ned again when he got back to the studio.

"There's someone I think you should see," Ned announced with bravado before Clarke had a chance to tackle him about Jane Etherington.

"Who?" Clarke asked, warily.

"Louise."

"Oh Christ, not Louise... Has she been looking for me?"

"Yeah. She's just blown into town. She wants to go to the funeral."

"Well, you can't very well stop her, Ned."

"No, but *you* can, Charlie. Look, can't you meet her and put her off the idea? Sure, if she comes, she comes. You're right... you can't stop anybody from going to a funeral. And I'm sure Jake would want all comers, but she is a bit of a handful. I was really thinking about Catherine. Mind you, she probably wouldn't mind, but it's just... Oh, you know what Louise is like, for God's sake. By the way, Charlie, I told her you'd meet her in Soho tonight... in the Blue Lamp... the small pub beside Berwick Street Market. Eight o'clock."

"Jesus, Ned! What the fuck did you do that for? Why the hell didn't you phone me first? I've had Jake's old flames up to here."

"I did call, but you weren't in your studio and your mobile's obviously buggered."

"Oh, fucking brilliant!"

"OK, Charlie, forget it, but if she comes to the funeral, she's your responsibility – right?"

"Why me?"

"Because you're the nice guy, Charlie. And you're her closest friend. Look, it's Friday, for Christ's sake. Just see what you can do."

16.

Charlie Clarke peeked round the bar door, repulsed by the brown leatherette sticking to his fingers like a clammy handshake, and wary of the nicotine smog threatening suffocation from the room beyond.

Searching through the smoke, his eyes found the familiar form of Louise McCall listing a degree further off beam than the last time he had seen her at one of the rash of weddings following graduation. Even then she tilted at a steady forty-five degrees to port. Louise McCall was rarely seen upright before pub opening time and never after closing.

Having sidestepped his way through the packed bar, Clarke slid up the worn banquette to fill the space beside her. He leant over, until he was parallel with her weeping-willow droop, to attract her attention, which, to judge by the rolling of her eyes, was dancing somewhere along the picture rail a foot below the ceiling.

"Hello, Loulou. It's me... Charlie."

"*Wa?*"

"Loulou. It's me... Charlie."

"*Wa?*"

"It's me, *Charlie.*"

"*Wa?*"

"Come on, Louise... it's Charlie. Oh for Christ's sake... it's Charlie Clarke. Charlie Clarke from St Martin's."

"St Martin's?"

"Yes. St Martin's School of Art."

"What the fuck are you doing here?"

"Well, I guess I came to talk to you... about Jake."

"Jake? Jake who?"

Louise McCall righted herself, straining her eyes to make some sense from a double vision of the busy bar room.

She had always been obstinate. He was never sure whether this was deliberate attention-seeking or whether she just operated on a different plane to everyone else.

"Jake Bloody McCullough."

"Oh, fuck off!" she said, listing again.

Her head hung so limply that her hair covered her face.

"Oh Jesus, Louise. What have you been doing to yourself?"

Suddenly she rose to the challenge and like a sleepy dog startled, she bit.

"Are you going to buy me a fucking drink or just sit there like the stuck-up prat you always were? It's a vodka and tonic. A bloody large one. Jesus, you can be a real pain in the arse, Charlie."

Clarke slid back across the banquette to make his way to the bar, grateful for the opportunity to reconsider his game plan.

When he returned to their dingy corner, he was relieved that the prospect of a fresh drink had elicited some semblance of life from Loulou McCall. How different she seemed, with her wiry frame and sunken eyes, to the very fresh-faced nineteen-year-old he had known at art college. Her once-red hair was now dull and flaxen like old straw, the large green eyes now browning like nicotine stains.

Suddenly, she was talking to him with a modicum of coherence.

"Jesus, you know, Charlie, I still miss Jake. I've missed him for years. Nobody has ever really filled the space... but it's funny, you know, now he's gone, I don't miss him at all."

Her words were starting to avalanche over the conversation and it was all he could do to make some sense from the snow.

"You know, he always sent me lilies on Valentine's Day."

"Lilies?"

"Shut the fuck up, Charlie..."

She would tolerate no interruption.

"Even this year, I got flowers on Valentine's Day," she continued. "And then on my birthday, he always sent me a book. You know, something he'd read. He always wrote a line or two inside the cover, nothing very romantic. He couldn't always make words work *that* spontaneously when it came to expressing his feelings; in fact, he could never express his feelings. He could talk for hours about what he knew, but about the way he felt... never."

"Did he love you, Louise?"

"Yeah, of course he fucking loved me. Trouble was he loved everybody else, too. He even loved his wife. Jesus, she put up with a lot. Yeah, he even loved her, but was he actually *in love* with any of us..? Oh, I don't know. He *was* a naughty boy, though."

"What do you mean?"

"Jesus, don't you know, Charlie?"

"Don't I know what? Oh, you mean he had a mistress?"

"Of course he didn't."

"Well, I didn't think so, but– "

"He had a string of them... a string of pearls."

"Are you sure?"

"Of course I'm bloody sure... I was one of them."

"What? When? Not recently? You don't mean you were still seeing Jake? Not after all this time?"

"Is the Pope a Catholic?"

"Did his... I mean... do you think his wife knew?"

"No, of course she didn't. Jake was far too crafty."

"Are you really sure about that?"

"Yep."

"And are you sure about the other women?"

"Of course."

"And was he still doing this until recently?"

"Yeah."

"How do you know?"

"I can't tell you."

"What?"

"I can't tell you."

"Look, Louise, I really need to know."

"OK," she said, pausing to add emphasis. "I fucked him last week, if you really want to know."

"You what?"

"You heard. I fucked him last week."

"No... Seriously?"

"Without a shadow of a doubt."

"You and he had sex last week?"

"Yep."

"Really?"

"Look, I was there, mate."

"Bloody hell. God, I hope Catherine doesn't find out."

"If I was you, Charlie, I wouldn't tell a soul. Forget about it, all right? Just forget about it. Please, forget about it."

Clarke gazed down into the blackness of his pint feeling sick.

"You know, the worst thing about finding out about Jake McCullough is... well... finding out about Jake McCullough. I'm starting to wonder what kind of person he really was."

"Look Charlie, who cares if he had mistresses. If they felt like I did when they were with him, then they were probably very happy. He was very charming. Great fun to be with. Always made me feel special. No one else ever bothered to do that. I mean, most people always treated me as a bit of a joke. Didn't they, Charlie?"

She looked at him accusingly.

"Well, I don't think– "

"Oh, come off it, Charlie, I know damn well," she said, leaning towards his face until the smell of stale alcohol and tobacco on her breath became unbearable. She was now too close to focus on, but close enough to kiss, and he wondered for a moment what she would do if he did.

"Louise?"

"*Wa?*"

"Please don't go to the funeral."

Louise swayed away from him, listing back to resume her original position, her hair tumbling over her face. And when she hadn't done or said anything for a minute, Clarke thought about nudging her in case she had fallen asleep.

"Why?" she said sharply, from the pit of her stomach, and then flicking her hair up and leaning back to stare at him once more.

"For his wife."

She sat suspended for a moment, majestic – savouring the power. And then from the depths of the well of all drink-driven obstinacy, bad temper and indecent behaviour, she nodded in affirmation.

Clarke hugged Loulou McCall, giving her a tender kiss before rolling her into a cab. As the taxi sped down the cobbled road and away from the pub, he watched her head bobbing in the rear window like a nodding dog's, and followed the cab's progress until it turned the corner of Broadwick Street.

Once out of sight he paused, took a deep breath, and then lit a fag. He ambled off with hunched shoulders and hands in pockets, blowing a plume of smoke high into the air.

Meandering through the debris of Berwick Street Market he made his way towards Wardour Street, pausing to kick out at a discarded cauliflower head. He wondered how Loulou would get out of the cab without him to prop her up.

The need to touch base with Ned sent him fumbling through his pockets for his mobile phone. He found it, shook it and then smacked it into the palm of his hand when it showed no signs of life. Frustrated, he delivered a *coup de grace* by flinging it into the clutter of cardboard boxes dumped around the next lamppost.

"Fuck it!" Clarke said under his breath, marching towards the row of red telephone boxes at the top of the alley leading through to Wardour Street. He phoned Finchley.

"Where are you, Charlie?" Ned asked, before Clarke could speak.

"You should bloody know."

"Yeah... right... Can you come over?"

"Look, I'm sorry, but I've got to say this. The eulogy, right, it's a waste of time. Right? I mean... I can't do it... I can't make him out... I mean... take anyone and look at their lives in microscopic detail... I mean... You can't... I mean... Making friends... It's a risky business... like buying an old car in an auction... They look nice and shiny when you first see them, but as soon as you get them home you notice bits of rust here, there and everywhere until you realise that the only bits of the car that aren't covered in rust are the tyres – and they're as bald as a baby's arse!"

"What the fuck are you babbling on about, Charlie? Just jump in a cab and come over."

"Why?"

"Why not? Come over for an hour. You deserve a drink."

"Look, Ned, there's time enough. I'll see you tomorrow night in Clove Rock."

"Actually, I've got something to show you I think you should see."

"Well, it's like this, Ned, I either get some work done tonight or I won't be going away tomorrow."

"Do you have a fax at work?"

"Yeah."

"What's your fax number?"

"The same as the phone. Why?"

"You'll see."

"Oh... Right."

"Anyway, how did you get on?" Ned said, trying to muster a tone of civility.

"All in all it's been a pretty shite day."

"It's been a pretty shite week... But you saw Louise?"

"Yeah."

"And?"

"Don't ask."

"OK. Call me later when you've seen my fax... Yeah? Make sure you do now. It's important."

If there was anything Clarke enjoyed less than working late at the studio he had yet to find it. One benefit – despite the cold, the gloom and the isolation – was that it encouraged him to work fast. There were no interruptions, no panicking clients phoning up with pernickety alterations or last-minute rush jobs. He would be in and out. It was still only half nine; he could be home and in bed by eleven, and then up, fresh and early, to get organised for the flight to Belfast in the afternoon.

Clarke pressed 'play' on the hi-fi, turned the volume up three digits in anticipation of the Elgar and sat down at his workstation and the large computer screen. At the touch of a button the hard disk blinked into life with its ever chirpy *pling*, barely audible over the opening bars of the *Cello Concerto*. Clarke double-clicked his mouse on the icon of the illustration software and called up the job in hand. A CD cover for a little-known country-and-western singer.

In the dim light of the late evening he was relieved to find the cover artwork looking as slick as when he had put it aside earlier in the afternoon. Clean, simple and professional. One hour and the illustration would be finished, and he could pop a proof into the post for his client on the way to the airport in the morning.

He was just applying some type when the phone rang. Irked by the distraction, he snatched at the receiver. There was no voice. It was the high-pitched scream of an incoming fax. *Shit*, he thought. He had forgotten to phone Finchley.

Clarke pressed the 'start' button and watched the paper roll through the black lips of the machine sitting on top of his monitor. The fax flowed down towards his lap in an unstoppable flow of A4, obscuring his view of the CD cover on the screen behind. It irritated him that he would now have to stop work to read it. The hour he had previously estimated would now be an hour and a half. In bed by twelve.

He tore the two-page fax across the lip of the machine and placed it on the desk in front of him. The top sheet was a handwritten note from Ned:

Charlie,
Cathy found this note in Jake's DJ when she got his effects

back from the hospital this morning. This was in his back trouser pocket. The dozy bastards at the hospital either didn't bother to look or just didn't find it, thank God!

Just shows you... Anyway, Cathy wanted you to see it.

Please dispose of the same when you have read it and, obviously, please keep this to yourself.

Cheers, Ned L.

The next sheet also comprised a handwritten note. Clarke recognised Jake's near-illegible prescription scrawl. From the black lines criss-crossing the paper he could tell that the note had been folded into four and bore what looked like a beer stain on one quarter, suggesting that until the last moment Jake had used his suicide note as a beer mat.

Dear Cathy,

By the time you read this... (You're supposed to open this kind of correspondence with words like these... are you not?)

Anyway, by the time you read this... I'll probably be down the pub and you'll probably have just collected my suit from the dry cleaners...

If that is the case... i.e. I am still alive and have failed in my objective, you should stop reading this note right now and throw it away (the note – not the suit).

No but... by the time you read this the chances are that I will be garbed head to foot in white chiffon and sitting on a cloud with a harp tucked under one arm.

I'm sorry I had to leave so soon, but I was kind of getting impatient... I was just sitting there having a few drinks on my own and I just thought... why not? You've tried most things, so why not this? So fine.

But do you know what the most annoying thing is? Do you know what I'm craving for right now, like I've never craved for anything else before... that I'd kill to get my hands on?

A fucking cigarette!

I haven't had a decent smoke in bloody years... Years... You'd think I could have one now... a man's last request and all that... I don't mind about the health risk... not now... and when you think about the agonies I went through to give up.

All reformed smokers should carry one cigarette... just one... sealed in a little glass case and hung on a chain round their necks... just in case of emergencies... always there – but untouchable – like those tiny hammers you get on underground trains... sealed behind glass... just for emergencies... just in case they're needed to smash the windows in a tube crash (if they're not already broken by the impact) or something like that...

Anyway, I digress.

Look, you know I love you... and I'm sorry if things do work out the way I've planned... i.e. I'm not in the pub... for I know you'll probably hate me for it – topping myself that is. But then again, you are the most understanding person I know, and so quick to forgive.

Please, please, please do three things for me. Firstly, tell the kids that I was a smashing bloke (even if you don't think it's true); secondly, come up with a good excuse for our friends and relatives to cover for my ridiculous behaviour, and thirdly... keep an eye on Ned for me.

Anyway, God bless... I've got to go now. I've got a bottle of vodka to down by four o'clock and the 4.30 from Kempton's due to start on the telly...

Big kisses, J xxx.

Clarke screwed up the note and hurled it into the bin by the door, raising his eyes in exasperation and struggling to suppress a smile. Thank God the authorities didn't find the note. Suicide would have ruined the funeral. *Bloody Jake McCullough,* he thought.

Clarke leaned over to the CD player. He had had enough of the Elgar *Cello Concerto*. The melancholy of the slow movement suited his mood too well. He put on the Beach Boys' *Pet Sounds* in the vain hope that its bland cheeriness would do the trick.

17.

Erroll Funk III sat slumped against the cold tube window, gleaning a little comfort from the vibrating pane as it massaged his scalp. He was gazing at the drizzle as it gyrated on the glass, fascinated by the heavier drops of rain wriggling to defy surface tension and break free. Here and there, they exploded into spindly streaks, colliding with and collecting the rainwater from others on the way – chaotic and directionless.

Funk followed the dervish dance through tunnels and round sharp bends, his concentration only broken when the watery maze was riven into a frenzied action-painting as the train braked hard on approaching another of the open-air stations on the Piccadilly Line.

"Damn the weather... and damn England," Funk cursed under his breath. It was never this dreary and depressing at home. The weather here was like the people – grey and unforgiving, lacking in character, heathen and ungodly.

He looked down the length of the carriage, checking the faces packed around him for confirmation. His revulsion for them made him feel shameful, uncomfortable that his head was so full of negative thoughts, and guilty that an enthusiastic evangelist of the gospels, such as he considered himself to be, could allow the pressures of life to overwhelm his normally irrepressible cheerfulness. He was ashamed that the inner flame of his faith, which had burned with such intense excitement on arrival at Heathrow Airport only two weeks before, flickered so feebly now.

Times had changed. The successful tour that Erroll Funk had anticipated, and for the most part of the trip enjoyed, had been overshadowed by the unfortunate events of the last week.

Two days previously he and the other twelve members of his gospel choir had participated in the final of a televised choral competition. It was intended to be the key engagement on the UK leg of their tour; the highlight and triumphant conclusion. However, the reality had proved a disappointment.

The trip had gone none too well since. The damp grey weather, with its continual rain, had not been anticipated and had worn them down; this was exacerbated by the realisation that their last engagement had been a PR disaster.

Now Funk questioned his motives. If the purpose of the Houston Seventh Day Tabernacle Gospel Choir was to spread The Word of The Lord, what the hell were they doing taking part in a singing competition? It was vanity, pure vanity. Theirs was a higher mission.

When they had been planning the trip back in Houston, and had voted to accept the invitation to enter the competition, he had suspected that it was a wrong and self-serving act but had done nothing about it. Nothing to dissuade the others. Nothing to stop it being written into the itinerary. For one who was proud of the sound of his own voice, Funk had kept very quiet. The group who had gathered to debate the subject at length, paused, contemplated the implications for no more than a few seconds and then scrambled their RSVP into the post.

They flew over to London excited by the challenge that the competition would bring, and happy that the free trip would help subsidise a string of public appearances – an opportunity to share the Good News.

Some of their concerts were modest, some high profile. And during the first ten days of the tour they revelled in the enthusiasm that their uproarious harmonised gospel singing elicited from a wide variety of audiences the length and breadth of Britain. They enjoyed the love showered upon them and could feel God's approval of their mission in the warmth of their reception, and could witness His beauty in the smiling faces of their audiences. They enjoyed the evangelising.

The first sign of discord came on the night of the literary awards event in Brighton. The choir's performance as the interval act was flawless, but the drunken behaviour of a few of their number in the free bar later caused disquiet. Unruly behaviour when alcohol is involved can be overlooked, but the effect on morale was soon compounded by the disappointing experience of the choral competition.

The competition need not have been the main event of their tour, but they had created a focus in their minds that had made it so. This wasn't evangelism. This was vanity, Funk now realised, and the vanity was what he regretted.

The inaugural *World Choral Challenge* was held on London's South Bank and attracted an eclectic ensemble of choirs from around the world. A Maori choir, the choir of the Red Army, a South African miners' choir, the NYPD choir, and so on.

The Houston Seventh Day Tabernacle Gospel Choir had rated their chance of success in the competition as high. They knew that their gutsy gospel had appeal in the host country, as experienced on their tour to date and in the glowing reviews their performances had generated on the arts pages of the broadsheets. They were also confident that the Lord would be willing them on from the wings – an all-powerful partner in the game of chance.

But then came the disappointment of the event.

The standard of competition was higher than they had anticipated. The judges had set a premium on technical excellence as opposed to character, and whilst the Tabernacle Gospel Choir had promised themselves a top three place before they had even sung a note – if not to win the darn thing – and although they qualified for the final with ease, they were unplaced in the judging.

The competition was won by the Treorchy Male Voice Choir, who relegated the Vienna Boys' Choir and the Canterbury Cathedral Choir School into second and third places.

The twelve guys from Houston were baffled. And now, sitting on the tube back to Heathrow watching the drizzle run down the carriage window, Erroll Funk felt resentful, and then guilty because of it.

"But goddamn, we were hot," he mumbled to himself. "And Jesus... those Welsh guys were so corny... And the schoolkids so syrupy... Where was their spirit? Where were their guts?"

As far as Funk was concerned the Tabernacle Choir had stolen the show, but where was their prize? That he was jealous was plain, but he just couldn't help himself. And that hurt too.

As Funk fought to get a clearer perspective, he took comfort that their mission could still be redeemed on the final leg of their tour. They had one week left to redress the balance with some wholesome evangelising.

Funk looked around the carriage at the mournful expressions worn by his colleagues. He decided that now was the time to lighten up and try to lift their spirits. The mixed bag of blue- and white-collar workers was reluctant to respond to Funk's winks and half-smiles at first, but the combination of his uncompromising determination and goofy grin gradually broke down the resistance of even the most stubborn; smiles bloomed again.

Encouraged by the changing atmosphere, Funk turned towards the large figure sitting on his right, and was about to make some light-hearted banter about the goddamn awful rain when a cockney accent, or what Funk took to be a cockney accent, crackled from the speaker above them:

"London Transport er... regret to inform customers er... travelling westbound on the Piccadilly Line, that the train er... travelling ahead of this one, has broken down in the underground section of the line between Earls Court and Barons Court stations.

"Er... London Transport apologises for any inconvenience caused to customers, and are doing everything within their power to clear the line at the earliest opportunity.

"Thank you."

"Goddamn," Funk cursed.

The train had already been standing for five minutes. Unfortunately, the driver had been stopped by a red light in the same stretch of tunnel as the broken-down train, rather than at the station before, which at least was above ground and, with the doors open, could offer a respite from the close atmosphere of a London Underground tunnel – hot and humid even in early autumn – and also the possibility of escape to continue by taxi.

Funk looked around him to attract the attention of the rest of the choir.

"What time's the plane?" Funk asked with authority, giving volume to his West-Virginian drawl and without directing the question to anyone in particular.

"5.30," Curly, the tall man next to him, answered abruptly.

"What's the goddamn time, Curly?"

"Four."

"Shiii-it," Funk cursed, rolling his eyes heavenward for dramatic effect, and decided to abandon his efforts to rally the morale of his men. "We ain't going to make it, are we?"

"Nope. It don't look like it."

Shit, " Funk repeated, rocking forward.

Funk sank back into his seat trying to suppress the rage bubbling close to the surface, and feeling particularly ungodly.

"Shit, shit, shit..," Funk swore quietly, glancing about him to see who would hear the expletives should his patience snap.

He checked on his group dispersed in ones and twos down the carriage, easily picked out in their bright red tour blazers and see-through plastic pacamacs. Most of the passengers, he guessed, were either tourists on their way to Heathrow or shoppers returning home from the West End.

"Does anybody know how long this goddamn train is going to be stuck here?" Funk demanded of his congregation.

The blond guy sitting on the bench seat opposite was looking straight back and talking to him. It made Funk jump. He was nervous of the locals. They rarely made conversation.

"We could be here for anything up to an hour," the blond guy said, folding his copy of the *London Evening Standard* to one side.

"Goddamn it!"

"May I ask where you're headed for?" Charles Clarke asked politely. He was happy to have someone to talk to, and had been fascinated by the red coats ever since they had boarded the train at Victoria.

"We've gotta catch the 5.30 flight to Belfast, Northern Ireland– "

"Oh, really?"

"Yeah, we're doing a TV chat show at 8.00... If we make it that is. We're a gospel choir," Funk said proudly, revealing a need for self-explanation Clarke thought typical of Americans abroad.

"Actually, I'm heading that way, too. The only thing in our favour is that if the whole of the Piccadilly Line is up the duff, there'll be plenty of others delayed for the flight. The airlines are pretty good at looking after their passengers when things like this happen. They usually know when there are hold-ups on the tube. Have you got a mobile? Phone them and let them know you might be a bit late."

"I don't have one. None of us do," Funk replied, shrugging.

"Oh, and mine's banjaxed, I'm afraid."

"Right..," Funk muttered, struggling to understand Clarke's colloquial English.

"Never mind... I can't see anybody else using one," Clarke said, surveying the carriage. "They don't always work down here, if they're working at all. Anyway, don't worry... the airline will know."

Funk leaned back in his chair sighing loudly and resigned to the catastrophe looming before them. He turned and pressed his brow against the cold window once more and let his eyes follow the thin lines of mortar running around the ceramic tiles of the tunnel walls.

Bored, Funk refocused his gaze inside the carriage, resting his eyes on what could be seen of the blond guy, re-submerged under his newspaper. As Funk read the front-page headlines, he became aware of a strange noise. He couldn't work out what it was or where it was coming from, but it sounded like moaning.

When he strained his ears, Funk decided that the noise was more of a hum than a moan. A very low, deep and gravelly hum. It seemed to be emanating from the depths of Curly's diaphragm. Funk detected the bass-line to one of the songs in their repertoire – a lament, a spiritual, and watched as Curly's gnarled lips quivered in mouthing the words; but quietly, quietly, so very quietly.

Funk caught Curly's attention, and winked in approval. Curly winked back, increasing the volume a notch. Curly hummed in a deep, basso profundo... *How could those idiot judges have overlooked Curly's beautiful voice?* Funk thought. It was unique, so pure and soulful – a little rough around the edges, but so much character.

Curly's humming, which was now audible above the idling train engine, seemed to galvanise others in the group. The altos added their voices then Ted, the tenor.

"Nobody knows the trouble I seen..," Ted sang, taking Curly's lead.

The others began to sing the words too, until all twelve members of the choir – now standing together in the doorwell halfway along the carriage – were united in the chorus. Funk joined them, stretching his arms wide to embrace as many as he could gather in his broad span, eyes beaming, his mood transformed.

Yes. The joy of the Lord is still with us, he thought. And his pride in the Lord lifted his voice and his spirit to a new plane of enthusiasm as he belted out the spiritual. The sound filled the crowded carriage and wafted over the passengers with the unrelenting surge of a riptide engulfing unwary onlookers.

Some passengers were startled as the booming chorus flooded down the carriage, thrown into a panic like trapped birds. Some faces reddened with embarrassment, unsure of what was expected of them. Payment? To join in? These, the minority, averted their eyes to their feet, or into newspapers, or up to the adverts running along the top of the carriage, and worried about what this spontaneous eruption was leading to. Handclapping?

The rest of the passengers were happy to register their approval by making eye contact with the singers, unafraid to be carried on the little tide of joy.

Having sung one song, and having found its voice, the choir moved onto another, upping the tempo as they did so, and slipping into their concert routine on autopilot. A tambourine was found.

Seizing the moment, the choir worked their audience with smiling eyes: reassuring the shy, coaxing the uncomfortable and teasing the unwilling. Funk felt God close at hand once more and beamed as he sang, laughing at the frailty of his own pride and thanking the Lord for showing him the error of his ways and for leading them to this time, this place, this opportunity to spread His word through their songs.

"Praise the Lord!" Funk shouted over the loud chorus, wearing a broader smile than he had for days.

And as they sang, they would have failed to notice the train move off, the obstruction cleared, save for the bumping and rolling as the driver let her go – keen as he was to finish the journey and get away home.

But the singing continued, and now even those who had been loath to enjoy the free concert were warming both to the performance and to the performers. There was no stopping the choir. They were euphoric.

As the train pulled into Barons Court Station, Funk was relieved to see other human life. *We must be singing at quite a volume,* he thought, judging by the surprised expressions of the people waiting on the platform as the carriage rolled alongside. Meanwhile, a glimpse of the station clock brought the welcome news that it was only 4.20pm. There was still time to catch the flight. Oh, God's light was truly shining on them once more. Hallelujah!

When the train came to a halt, the choir was silent, squeezing to one side to let passengers off and make space for those stepping aboard. The carriage doors were just sliding shut and the Tabernacle Choir bracing themselves to belt out another number, when two pairs of hands sprang like grappling hooks from the platform into the fast-narrowing gap. The hands seized the rubber binding on the edge of each door and started to force them open again. Two men in uniform then squeezed their way aboard through the small aperture by rotating off one another like the rollers on a mangle. Once inside, the doors clunked shut behind them.

Their uniforms were of an ill-fitting concrete grey and topped off with an officious-looking cap. Enamel badges identified them as London Underground ticket inspectors.

Clarke was eyeing them suspiciously, expecting nothing more than the slight inconvenience of having to rummage through his pockets for his ticket, when the shorter of the two pulled the emergency handle. The train stopped with a sharp jerk. The short one then turned towards the Tabernacle Gospel Choir, facing down his prey like a pit bull, squat and powerfully built.

Meanwhile the other inspector, tall and gawky, bowed his head to talk into the radio clipped to his lapel. Clarke looked on, wondering what the problem could be, but unable to hear what was being said. The choir stood bewildered; the pit bull focusing far down the carriage to avoid eye contact, the tall inspector looking as though he wished he were invisible.

The carriage doors reopened.

"Thanks Dave," the tall one squawked into his lapel with added confidence. He positioned himself beside the pit bull. Brains beside brawn.

"OK... you lot. Off the train now, thank you," The pit bull growled, herding the choir through the doors with outstretched arms.

"Hey! Just hang on one darn minute– " Funk protested, but to no avail, as the bulk of the choir was already bending to the will of the inspectors. Funk was left with no option but to follow.

Within seconds they were all off the train and standing on the platform amid a sea of suit bags and hand baggage, with the doors of the tube train sliding shut behind them. Inside, Clarke stood up and made a dash towards the doors, thinking that maybe he could intervene on behalf of the singers. It was too late, however; the doors beat him. The train was already moving off. Clarke stood helpless, with the palms of his hands and his forehead pressed tight against the glass, watching the gaggle of Texans shrinking from view.

The singers rallied for a counter-attack, surrounding the two guards who were dwarfed and outnumbered. From the distance, Clarke could see that the choir was growing more vociferous as it closed in on its tormentors – stirred from the torpor of the long tube journey by the rude interruption. Clarke caught a last glimpse of Erroll Funk, great arms flailing aloft and getting angry.

"Jesus! What was that all about?" Clarke asked the small man in the Burberry mac who had been sitting next to him for most of the journey. But there came no reply, just an embarrassed smile. Moments earlier, Burberry Man had been clapping along with the choir. Now, he could offer little more than an awkward smile with eyes averted. God, he's reverted to type, Clarke thought, *typical bloody commuter.*

Clarke slunk back into his seat, picked up his newspaper, looked at it briefly, had second thoughts and hurled it onto the empty seat opposite, too preoccupied with the human condition to read.

What the hell had those guys been doing that had so upset the London Underground authorities, anyway? Surely, they had paid their fares? They must have made some silly mistake. Tourists always do, he thought. Oh well, not his problem... *But Jesus! What a terrible advert for London,* he muttered to himself, tutting loudly.

Clarke leaned back, drifting off into a daydream. He was so glad to be getting out of the rainy city. Glad to be getting away from his desk, his studio, his routine. For the first time, he started to contemplate what it would be like to be back in Northern Ireland. The thought pleased him. He had fallen in love with the Province the first day he arrived for college twenty years ago. It was the people. He had spent most of his childhood in London and although he liked London, he didn't like the insularity of Londoners. They weren't the world's greatest talkers. By contrast, he found Belfast people open, generous and talkative. In fact, they never seemed to shut up. He also liked that Belfast was close to the countryside. It was easy to get away from the smoke, to escape to the coast or the hills, to the Glens of Antrim, the Causeway Coast, or Donegal.

Not even his reservations about the funeral could dispel his eagerness to be back in Northern Ireland. Jake's funeral was sure to bring the misery of the last week to a head. Once out of the way, he assumed life would begin to return to normal. He smiled at the thought of normality, clueless as to what that might be.

18.

It's twelve minutes and twenty-three seconds past five. The high-speed ferry from Stranraer to Belfast is due to depart at 5.15pm. The last of the cars has been loaded with military precision and the ship's engines are idling and ready to go. At the stern, the ramp quivers as its hydraulic pistons throb in anticipation of the massive charge of electricity soon to draw it up.

A stone's throw down the quay, four men in black overcoats have emerged from a hearse, and are struggling towards the ferry as fast as their load will allow – their knees angry, their ankles inflamed. They are manhandling an XL coffin which, because of their hurry, looks in danger of receiving a premature burial at sea. A few yards to go and the lead man is waving, a desperate signal imploring patience to anyone onboard who might see.

They are in luck. The chief engineer has spotted their progress and, because he is curious, waits for them to scuttle down the slipway and onto the boat before pressing the green button to raise the ramp.

The ramp shudders before commencing its juddering ascent. This alerts the men in black, who shout frantically, and with scant regard for decorum, deposit the coffin on the ground, turn tail and make a run for freedom, jumping onto the concrete slipway – about a four-foot drop from the boat – before they are carried out to sea. Ashore, they turn to watch the ship as it glides out of its berth. One man is panting, two are exchanging curses and the fourth rocking with laughter. They are then sent into another frenetic dance as the first wave from the ship's wash comes ashore and chases them up the slipway.

On board, the coffin is left where it lies beside a bulkhead, but is secured with a yellow tie that will act like a seat belt, the irony of which is not lost on the deckhands, who shrug at one another – a form of communication encouraged by the loudness of the ship's engines. Albert Lewis is bound for Ireland. The box, incongruous amongst the parked cars, is a disturbing omen like the company of an albatross or the sight of a lone magpie on a rainy day.

19.

Charlie Clarke was in a hurry. What with the hold-up between Earls Court and Barons Court stations, and the delay when the Texans were thrown off the train, time was now tight – possibly too tight – for him to catch his plane. He stood by the carriage door shuffling his feet, glancing through the glass and then back at his watch every ten seconds, willing the hands to slow down and the station to come into view, constantly reassessing his chances.

The window was cold, but by pressing his cheek hard against the pane, he could see the platform lights in the distance as the train approached the long straight before the station. The Terminal One stop seemed to have taken hours to reach compared with the one or two minutes between the other stations on the line. For a moment, he enjoyed the feel of the cold glass on his clammy skin.

As the train pulled alongside the platform, Clarke pumped the 'open door' button, even though he knew it had no chance of working until the train had stopped. Not that he was in a panic; just didn't want to miss his flight, and wanted to give catching it his best shot.

As soon as the doors slid open, he was out and running across the platform heading for the 'up' escalator, bag in hand and then thrown over one shoulder for the sprint down the labyrinth of corridors that lay between him and the ticket desk.

Clarke slowed to a jog when he reached the departure lounge, which was as fast as his tight lungs and heavy case would allow. He rued the last ten years of smoking. Running to the ticket desk, running to the banks of check-in desks, running to the gate, running to the boarding point – it was only when he handed his boarding card over to a stewardess and could see the queue of passengers just ahead of him and still filing down the gangway into the nose of the plane, that he felt he could afford to walk. A sigh and then gasps for air, discarding as much loose clothing as could be carried under one arm together with his hand baggage.

Once on the plane, Clarke dropped into his seat, leant his head back and took a deep breath.

"God, what a life," he murmured through gritted teeth.

He sat taking deep breaths, trying to relax, unwinding his fingers, splaying them out from the tight fists that they had become and feeling the tension ease. *Practice what you preach,* he thought, chastising himself when he remembered the laid-back attitude he had assumed to reassure the Americans on the tube.

Clarke closed his eyes to shut out the bustling of the cabin crew busybodying about him. He couldn't bring himself to look out of the window – sick of the sight of drizzle. The rain was still pouring from clouds which had stained the sky mauve. He prayed that there wasn't anybody else on board flying out for the funeral, as he relished the hour of peace that the short flight would bring before the inevitable pandemonium at Breige's house.

Clarke looked at his watch. The plane seemed to have been sitting on its stand a long time.

"Excuse me, sir..."

A large breathless figure was looming over him.

"I appear to have the window seat," the large figure continued.

"Oh, right. No problem."

Clarke shook himself out of his lethargy and rose to let the passenger squeeze past.

"Jesus, it's you!" Clarke exclaimed. "I didn't think you'd make it."

"Well, it was touch and go," Erroll Funk replied, still panting.

"Charlie Clarke. How do you do?"

Clarke offered a warm smile.

"Erroll Funk III. Pleasure to make your acquaintance, sir."

Funk assaulted Clarke with a bone-crunching handshake.

"What the hell happened to you back there?"

"'Hell' is the word, Mr Clarke. Hell, the Devil and the London Underground. Those kind gentlemen seemed to have mistaken us for buskers, which apparently is a crime second to none in your city, sir. They didn't seem to understand that we are on a mission... But we put them straight."

"Er, how?"

"Buskers don't usually carry evening dress in suit bags. We also didn't have any loose change to show for our efforts. That and... well, somebody happened to recognise us from the TV and put in a good word... HEY CURLY! HURRY IT UP, MAN!" Funk shouted without warning as the rest of the team appeared. Funk, if nothing else, was loud.

"Well, I'm sorry about that," Clarke interjected. "I can only apologise on behalf of London Transport... But I wish I could have done some– "

"I saw you. Don't worry, man... CURLY... KEEP YOUR HAIR ON! DON'T GO BUMPING INTO THOSE NICE LADIES!" Funk boomed as the choir's basso profundo clattered past the stewardesses at the top of the aisle, thumping them with his shoulder bag.

"TV?" Clarke asked.

"I'm sorry?"

"What TV?"

"Oh, we did a couple of shows... A National Lottery thing and an awards."

"The National Lottery Show?"

"Yeah... backing vocals for a young pop star who wanted to add a bit of spice to his act. You know, a bit of soul... a gospel choir. Oh, it was fine. You know... the folks seemed to love it. Nice kid too. Wants us to sing on his next CD. We're still fashionable apparently."

"And now Northern Ireland?"

"If we make it, that is. Following the TV show tonight, we're playing the Waterfront Hall, Belfast tomorrow; The Guildhall, Londonderry, Monday; The Point, Dublin, Tuesday and Wednesday; and then back home stateside on Thursday."

"You're busy enough, then?"

"It's the Lord's work, Mr Clarke."

"Mmm... I'm sure."

Clarke hoped he wasn't going to get drawn into a hard sell, but was saved as the air stewardesses took to the floor for the synchronised safety demonstration, the walk past to make a final head count, and the check to ensure that seat belts are worn and tables stowed away. Clarke looked at Erroll Funk out of the corner of his eye, trying to calculate his age. Early fifties? Maybe fifty-two or -three? He wore a bit of weight around his face with a hint of jowl under the cheeks. He was getting a tad tubby all round, but there was no disguising that up until recently he must have been a handsome man. A hint of his looks was still there: unlined features dominated by a razor-sharp smile.

"What is the purpose of your visit? Are you from Northern Ireland?" Funk asked as the plane taxied forward onto the runway.

"No. I'm from Dublin. Well... at least, my parents are."

"And?"

"And what?"

"Why Northern Ireland?"

"Er... actually, I'm going to a funeral."

"Oh, I'm sorry."

"It's OK."

"Were they old?"

"No, no. About my age. About thirtysomething."

"Hey, I'm sorry."

Funk pulled what he hoped was a serious expression.

"That's OK."

Funk paused to make sure that his next question was well phrased.

"Were they ill?"

124

"No, they topped themselves, actually," Clarke whispered from behind his left hand, hoping that his bluntness would put an end to the conversation. It didn't.

"Suicide?"

"Yeah."

"Oh man, that's terrible."

There was no stopping Funk now.

"Yes, very shocking. He wasn't one of those you would worry about in that way... you know?"

"Yeah. I do know. It's not uncommon."

Clarke didn't want to go over the whole saga again, but there was something engaging about Funk and his childlike curiosity. Reluctantly, Clarke retold Jake's story. Already, the telling was becoming formulated into something like a script. He wanted it over. But then the engines revved, drowning the monologue. They sat in silence as the plane hurtled down the runway for take-off. The longer the silence lasted, the harder it became to make meaningful conversation again.

The rain appeared to increase in intensity as they accelerated into the drizzle. Erroll Funk watched the raindrops blur on the window again as the plane sped into the gloom and thought of the sunshine at home. Airborne, they banked into a steep curve heading away from London, north towards Liverpool and the Irish Sea.

"So why did he do it?"

"God, you like to ask leading questions, don't you? ...I don't have a clue. Well, all I have is clues, but they don't come together to create a very coherent picture, I'm afraid. It turns out he was leading something of a double life."

"Mmm... He sounds interesting. Was he religious, by any chance?"

"Jesus, what the hell's religion got to do with anything?" Clarke asked irritably.

"God's got something to do with everything, man. Where does He fit into your life?"

"He doesn't. Somewhere in last place, behind Father Christmas, the Easter Bunny and the Tooth Fairy."

"You're not a believer then, I take it?"

"No. Very few of us who survived an education at the hands of the Christian Brothers are."

"Oh, so you don't approve of religion?"

"Look... it's not that simple. I mean... just because I don't believe in Santa Claus doesn't mean to say that I don't love the guy. I do... and I love God. I love the idea of Him... It's just that I don't buy the theology, I'm afraid."

"Maybe it's not a good subject for you right now– "

"Actually I think God hates us. Maybe that's why we die. He created a beautiful world, but ran out of ideas when it came to designing its people... that's why he made us in his own image. He didn't know what else to do. But then when he had a good look he was startled by what he saw – like me or you catching a glimpse of ourselves in a shop window on a bad hair day. Changed his mind then and there. Decided to get rid of the lot of us and start over. Only problem... he was exhausted from creating the world. He couldn't do it in one go and didn't have the formula for how. He still hasn't quite figured it out. So he's just picking us off one by one... waiting till we're old and frail and it's easier. Let's face it... sometimes he has a sudden burst of energy when he's firing on all cylinders – like a good war or a bit of genocide – but generally he can only get us one by one. We'd live forever otherwise. God's a serial killer. He's been murdering us for years."

"Friend, you are warped."

"Just imaginative."

"Yours is a frightening mind."

"Good. Now maybe you'll leave me be for a while."

The two men sat in silence avoiding small talk for the moment.

"Maybe your friend was ill."

Funk couldn't contain himself for long.

"So?"

"So maybe there was nothing you could do."

"Look... What are you trying to say?"

"That life is hard enough without having to carry a burden of guilt on your shoulders. That's what religion can do for you... It's great for absolution. But then maybe you don't need that. Maybe I'm wrong. Maybe you're OK."

"What would make you think otherwise?"

"Your face."

"What about it?"

"You look... You look... Oh, never mind."

"What?"

"Guilty. Guilty and sad."

Clarke raised his eyebrows. He wasn't playing ball. To telegraph his waning interest, he picked up the in-flight magazine and flicked through the pages. Funk sighed in resignation.

20.

Albert Lewis would have felt more than a little self-conscious arriving in Belfast on the 5.15 ferry from Stranraer. It would have been his first visit to Northern Ireland and he would have been nervous. It was overcast and Saturday. He would have been impressed by the city, though, and surprised by the pleasant views down the lough and of the surrounding hills. However, his meeting with the sombre reception committee – there to collect his remains and transport them the last forty miles to Clove Rock – would have induced a rare shyness. He would have felt uncomfortable that his reticence did not do justice to his outgoing personality.

The serious, unsmiling professionalism of the funeral parlour staff would have irked him. He liked warm faces, and always offered a friendly smile himself to put others at ease. The poker-faced seriousness of these men would have thrown him off balance, made him quiet and withdrawn.

Though this was Albert's first time in Northern Ireland, it wasn't his first visit to Ireland. In his twenties, before the war, he had roamed the West of Ireland on summer holidays, having taken a week off work to cycle or take the train through Galway and Connemara.

He loved the beaches – sweeping bands of yellow, fringed by smooth slabs of black and grey rock. And when he was out walking on some rocky outcrop or on the shore and came across a particularly beautiful stone, and if he judged it to be the right size – slightly bigger than a house brick would do – he would prise it from the landscape, put it in a cardboard box, wrap it in brown parcel paper, tie it with string and send it home to 120 St Leonard's Road, Hove, courtesy of the penny post.

Often, he would arrive back at the house before his parcel, and would be looking through the curtains as the postman struggled up the garden path with the contraband. While some people collected postcards, mugs or tea towels as souvenirs, Albert collected rocks which, over time, he built into a rockery in his front garden – a monument to his time in Ireland, the pillage of his favourite country, the significance of which went unnoticed by his suburban neighbours.

Jake's sisters were in Belfast to meet the coffin, sign for the remains and to ensure that there were no cock-ups. Albert would have taken a shine to the two dark-haired girls with deep sparkling eyes and full figures, but today he would have kept his distance, such was their grief.

Albert's coffin was carried off the ferry to the waiting funeral car with care. Once the coffin was rolled into position, the Clove Rock funeral director, Donal Magee, shepherded the girls, Sinéad and Orla, into his wife's family saloon. Everyone in place, Magee climbed in beside the driver of the hearse and donned his silk-trimmed topper. He was a traditionalist.

Magee hoped that the traffic between the ferry terminal and the motorway would not be too heavy. He hated driving through town traffic, knowing how irritated drivers in the city would be when held up by the small cortege poodling along at no more than twenty miles an hour. They had to travel at that speed. It was expected. It was respectful. It was tradition. But it was also more than likely to cause a multiple car crash borne of the impatience of other drivers determined to overtake at any cost. Like the cut of men's trousers, the creaminess of milk, and the price of a pint, respect for the dead wasn't what it was, Magee thought. There was a time, he remembered, when no one would overtake a hearse.

21.

The flight to Belfast was brief – about an hour and a quarter. By the time that the in-flight meal had been served, eaten and cleared, the plane was descending towards the City Airport on the western shore of Belfast Lough. Clarke's view of the approach over the giant yellow cranes of the Harland and Wolff shipyard and the terraced streets of East Belfast was obscured by Erroll Funk's fidgeting in the window seat beside him. Funk was oblivious to the cityscape below as he fiddled with an assortment of papers, either lifting them out of, or stuffing them back into the brown leather shoulder bag at his feet.

The passengers in row eighteen, seats A and B, hadn't exchanged a word since the arrival of the prefabricated lunch, after which Clarke slept through the rest of the flight until the descent. Silence had now gripped the other passengers, save for the crying of a baby whose wails rose higher in volume the lower the aircraft flew; those within earshot fought hard to sustain a strained smile.

On landing, Clarke's escape was swift. For once he was lucky in the roulette of baggage collection. Wandering through to the conveyor belt, his cheap green travel bag had already been regurgitated, so that he merely had to scoop it up as he sauntered by.

He felt pricked by loneliness on the main concourse amidst the human kerfuffle of excited reunions and tearful goodbyes. As he ambled over to airport information, however, he was relieved to catch sight of Ned Labinski leaning against the desk, car keys in hand.

"Jesus, Ned. It's good to see you."

Clarke hugged him with his free arm.

"You too. You too."

"Thanks for coming to get me."

"No problem. Breige lent me her car. Anyway, it's good to get away from the house for a while."

"Oh. Are things getting hairy?"

"No, not too bad. Though Christ knows what it'll be like tomorrow for the wake."

Looking back over his shoulder Clarke caught a last glimpse of Erroll Funk. He was engaged in banter with a mass of nuns at the baggage carousel. Then the automatic doors separating 'Arrivals' from the entrance hall slid shut to obscure the view.

Outside, the air was laced with a heavy scent wafting from the lough shore. It reminded Clarke of childhood trips to the seaside and the smell of shingle and seaweed.

"Good old Belfast – it doesn't change much," Clarke mumbled into the strong wind.

"*Wha?*"

"BLOODY WEATHER!" Clarke shouted.

"Oh well... No one comes to Ireland for sunshine. Anyway, it's good pub weather!"

"Is anyone else here yet?"

"Not that I've seen. Was there anyone on your flight?"

"I don't think so. Mind you I don't know if I would recognise any of them these days, Ned."

"Sure."

"Well, we probably won't see anyone 'til the funeral service. I told them all to stay at one of those Travel Lodge places in Templepatrick. It's handy for the airport, but still far enough away from Jake's mum's. Anyway, I think most of them are travelling over tomorrow."

"Thank God."

"What?"

"THANK GOD!"

Ned had parked opposite the exit. Clarke was pleased to get on the road.

"Fancy a drink before we get there?"

"Not half," Clarke answered with enthusiasm.

"We'll have a pint, then... Where do you reckon?"

"We might as well get out of the city and head west. We'll get a drink nearer Jake's."

Clarke still knew the territory.

As they drove onto the dual carriageway heading for the M2, they passed through the east of the city. Clarke leaned closer to the window for a better view. Staring out at Belfast, he was surprised by the volume of redevelopment. There had been a dramatic change in the cityscape since his last visit. He had always thought that Belfast resembled Liverpool – red brick and Victorian. Now, he thought it looked more like Croydon – grey and high-rise.

One thing that hadn't changed though, the colour coding: the Loyalist red, white and blue kerbstones of East Belfast and the Republican tricolours flying from the tower blocks to the north. Parts of the city where every day is either a royal jubilee or St Patrick's Day.

22.

"Are you ready for this, Charlie?" Ned mumbled, semi-anaesthetised by a couple of pints.

"What? The funeral?" Clarke asked, feeling disinclined to broach the subject.

"Have you worked out what you're going to say yet?"

"Why?"

"No reason."

They paused while Ned ordered another round of stout.

Two pints down and twenty miles from Clove Rock, Ned Labinski and Charlie Clarke were sitting at the bar of the Three Keys Inn on the Castledawson Road, which like Bates' Motel in *Psycho* had been bypassed by modern times and a new dual carriageway. Custom at the old pub had been maintained, however, by renovation and the introduction of a vast menu, served all day, fresh from a microwave.

They were sitting in the snug in preference to the new lounge bar, whose sterile refurbishment had cleaned through the old interior with the clinical efficiency of bleach. Labinski and Clarke felt more at home in the old bar. The tatty Formica tables, red vinyl stools and nicotine veneer smacked of authenticity and generations of hard drinking. Its dirt talked history.

"Maybe the eulogy wasn't such a good idea, Ned."

"Oh God, not the eulogy again! What the hell's the matter now?"

"Jane Etherington for starters."

Clarke uttered her name with slow emphasis, emboldened by a grasp of the nettle.

"What about her, Charlie?"

"Who is she, exactly?"

"You know. You met her."

"Of course I know who she *is*, Ned, but where does she fit in... with Jake I mean... What do you know that I don't? And why are you looking so nervous?"

"Am I?"

"Yes, you are, actually. And tell me, Ned... tell me about Loulou McCall, while we're at it."

"Look, Charlie, you know you can take 99.9% of whatever she says with a pinch of salt."

"Funny. You said the same of Jane Etherington. Anyway, how do you know what Loulou said? I haven't had a chance to tell you."

"I don't. But I can guess. I know what she's like. Anyway, what *did* she tell you that's got you so edgy?"

"That she and Jake had been fucking about for years. That Jake had been fucking about for years."

"Well, Charlie, you don't need me to tell you that that's absolute bollocks, do you?"

"Are you sure? Do you really know, Ned? I mean do you really know what was going on? I haven't a clue myself, and trying to get a straight answer from someone... anyone... from you... is proving pretty difficult. I can tell there's something not quite right. I mean, what is there to hide?"

"What? You think that there's a cover-up? Oh, don't be daft, Charlie."

"Well? What *is* going on?"

"Look... you're not a bloody detective. Catherine has only asked you to say a few words at a funeral."

"She told me to find out about him!"

"She only meant you to get a few pointers so you'd have something to say. You're not heading a judicial inquiry. You're not a detective on a murder case. Don't get things out of proportion. Why do you think Catherine asked you to do the eulogy in the first place?"

"Well, actually... I think she said it was because she thought I would be good at it."

"Yeah, yeah, yeah... and I wouldn't want to do it... blah, blah, blah. Do you want to know the real reason?"

"What?"

"No.... maybe– "

"Oh, just tell me, for God's sake!"

"Well, she thought you would need something to do."

"What the hell does that mean, Ned?"

"OK. She was worried about you."

"What?" Clarke said, sitting up straight.

"She was worried about how you would cope in light of what's happened. You know– "

"Look, you can say it, Ned."

"OK ...about what happened to your kids."

"They have names, Ned."

"...To Alex and Holly."

"Alex and HEATHER."

"I mean Heather. Sorry."

They both took a swig of beer. The pause felt awkward.

"You know this really pisses me off, don't you, Ned?" Clarke said, slamming down his pint.

"Well, no. I don't know, to be honest."

"So you're trying to tell me that Catherine asked me to do the eulogy because she was worried that I might crack up if I didn't have something to keep me busy?"

"Yeah... No. Oh, I don't know... She cares for you... and so do I."

"Oh God, Ned. Do you know how bloody patronising that sounds? And I thought I was doing this for your sake. If you really want to know what my problem is, it's that no one will ever talk to me about them. No one, but no one, dares speak to me about the children. And especially not Kay. That's what split us up, eventually. We couldn't talk about it. And, of course, I'm dying to talk about them... What they looked like, the funny things that they did, the fun we had... but everyone's too bloody cautious. No one wants to risk hurting my feelings. As a result, I'm avoided like the effing plague and my memory of the kids is disappearing into a quicksand of silence. I mean... doing Jake's bloody eulogy is hardly going to swing the balance, is it?"

Clarke was leaning forward and staring into Ned's face. Ned looked away.

"Calm down. She cares about you. She was worried. That's all."

"Yeah... maybe."

"Tell me," Ned said, looking up.

"What?"

"Tell me about the children."

"Oh, I can't be bothered now."

"No... do..."

"No. Not now. But I'll tell you what, Ned... Fuck the damn eulogy."

"Oh, come on... Let's face it, you're the only one who can do a good job. And that's all that matters."

"Maybe... but what about Jane then, Ned?"

"Jane Etherington?"

"Yes."

"What about her?"

"Where does she fit in? She told me you'd tell me, by the way."

"Did she?"

"Yeah."

"Look, Charlie, there's little mystery there. She was just someone that Jake met at work. She was a friend."

"What kind of friend, Ned?" Clarke asked, leaning even closer.

"A friend. It's not very complicated."

"So why the mystery?"

"There's no mystery."

"Well, I'd never heard of her before this week."

"Sure, but then you haven't been around that much over the last few years, Charlie. We all meet new people. We've all moved on a bit... widened our circle. What do you expect?"

"Of course... but I've just got a feeling about her and Jake."

"Well, take it from me there's nothing there. You can be sure of that."

Ned placed a hand on Clarke's arm to reassure him.

"Well, I'm not totally convinced."

Ned didn't reply, but downed what was left of his pint.

"Come on, Charlie. Let's go whilst I'm still fit to drive."

Half an hour later, Ned flicked the indicator to turn onto the back road to Breige McCullough's home – a large detached bungalow standing in its own grounds and reached by a private lane.

As Ned negotiated the twisty drive, the car, the drive, and the house, which first appeared as a grey blot on a greyer landscape, were drenched in bright halogen. A vast eighties' bungalow, the house was still raw with newness. Ned thumped the horn as they pulled up. Breige popped out of the front door with the deftness of the woman in a weatherclock when the day turns sunny.

Having greeted them with enthusiastic hugs, Breige bustled them through into the kitchen where the family's womenfolk were gathered around the table. There was something of a party atmosphere; spirits were being lifted. The kitchen table, which filled the majority of the floorspace, was festooned with empties.

Clarke noticed Sinéad McCullough gazing at him. Nothing new. He could feel his cheeks blushing red and cautioned himself not to be self-conscious. But there was an intensity to Sinéad's expression that induced a momentary shiver of anticipation.

But why would she think anything of you? an inner voice taunted, encouraging him to believe he was mistaken.

"Where's Gerry and Connor?" Clarke asked.

"We sent them up to the town for a game of pool," Sinéad replied.

Clarke thought it strange that Jake's brothers were never around. A testimony to the size of Irish families – so big they could rarely be accommodated in any one room at the same time.

"We've had people stampeding through here all afternoon, Charlie. It was very tiring. We sent the boys away to let off steam.

They've been locked up with Holy Joes all day – present company excluded," Orla added, between slurps from a large glass of wine.

"We had a prayer vigil this evening. There were some very long faces," Breige continued.

Clarke suddenly realised that Jake's coffin would be somewhere in the house, and that tomorrow the town would be passing through to view his corpse. How ghoulish, he thought.

"What can I get you two to drink?" Breige asked, more composed than when Clarke had visited her in London. Maybe it was easier to cope now that she was home. She was also sober, which set her apart from the rest of the room.

Catherine was standing on the far side of the table leaning against the Aga. She acknowledged Clarke with a wink, which unsettled him, not knowing what it meant nor how to respond. His confidence was draining fast and he felt disoriented and dizzy. At thirty-five years of age, he could still be excruciatingly shy.

He gave Catherine one of his lopsided smiles, which he hoped was friendly, but knew, because he had been told, often appeared cold and miserly. Catherine seemed calm, though he imagined her composure was a smokescreen. If he hadn't felt so ill at ease, he would have enveloped her in a bear hug, but his head was spinning and the dizziness made the few yards to the other side of the room look a marathon.

"Where are the kids?" Clarke mouthed.

"In bed," Catherine mimed, placing her hands to the side of one cheek as she bent her head.

Breige poured two glasses of Guinness. Clarke was relieved to see that a healthy number of the women were smoking. Thank God, he thought, that Northern Ireland was still a safe haven for smokers. The air was stifling.

"Charlie... this is my friend Roisin from up the road... and Deirdre – Jake's cousin... Ann Thompson and her daughter Lizzie... and these are Jake's aunts – Margaret and Patsie."

Breige pranced around her guests: tipsy women with red-veined faces who beamed at Clarke, encouraging his already radish-coloured cheeks to burn beetroot. He raised his glass and smiled as best he could.

"Now, you help yourself to a few drinks. It'll warm you up for the wake tomorrow," Breige whispered into Clarke's ear.

Ned had already worked his way round to the other side of the table and was chatting to Sinéad and Orla. Meanwhile, Clarke was getting dragged into conversation with the Thompsons.

Fuelled by his fourth pint, Clarke found conversation easy enough at first, but soon felt awkward around people with whom he had little in common. He hadn't anticipated this level of petty socialising back in London.

His eyes kept straying away from Mrs Thompson and her daughter and across the room to Ned, who was chatting to Sinéad and Orla; he was envious that Ned had monopolised the attention of the girls, who, with every sip of Guinness, seemed more alluring and less attainable.

Though he tried hard to concentrate on whatever polite conversation the Thompson women were making, they could not hold his attention for long. They were friendly enough, but were not talking about Jake, Catherine, Ned, Jane Etherington or any of the other personalities who were central to the funeral and prominent in Clarke's thoughts. And he couldn't help noticing how dull the Thompson daughter appeared. Not in looks, but in character. She said little except to give assent to anything and everything her mother had to say. And the more the mother talked, the less Clarke paid attention. She was trying to entertain him with a detailed account of everything she knew about the South of England and the achievements of her son Matthew, who was studying at Exeter University and evidently an academic marvel.

Breige caught Clarke's attention as she squeezed past, raising her eyebrows at him in sympathy. Clarke was rooted to the spot, stunned by a combination of alcohol and tedium. His anxiety to get away and talk to a sympathetic soul tore at his chest. Above all, he needed to talk about Jake.

Clarke kept drifting off into deep thought, unable to square what Ned had been telling him in the pub with the weight of preconception that had been building all week. Ned's reassurances just didn't wash. And still Mrs Thompson twittered on...

"Have you been to Northern Ireland before?"

"Well, yes... er... I met Jake at college here."

"Oh, what did you study?"

"Art and design," Clarke replied, economising on words as far as possible.

"Matthew was very good at art at school, but we persuaded him that engineering would suit him better."

"Why didn't he go to Queen's?"

"Queen's, Belfast?"

"Yes."

"He wasn't keen. We were never quite sure why," Mrs Thompson replied in a ponderous voice. "But Exeter is red brick," she added, regaining her enthusiasm.

"Sure," Clarke mumbled, now distracted by the Thompson daughter. He decided that she had a certain prettiness – a good bone structure and clear blue eyes with an allure that suggested she knew more than she dared say. Clarke perceived that she was as much a captive in Breige's kitchen as he.

Warming to her, he let his eyes search for the outline of her breasts and hips, hidden by the frumpy jumper and billowing skirt swamping her silhouette. His eyes scanned the length of her crossed legs down to her ankles – always a good indicator of overall physique, he thought. They were finely chiselled, with a long angular joint. He approved.

Given the opportunity, he fantasised, would she escape with him? Just get up and leave, take a car and make a dash for the border. Donegal. Just the two of them. And he could see it in her eyes, urging him, daring him to do it – right there, right now.

Snapping himself awake from the daydream, he found he had to cross his legs to conceal the bulge growing in his trousers, aware that he was probably blushing an onion purple.

"And what do you do, Mr Clarke?" Mrs Thompson asked him.

"Er... I design children's books. I also illustrate them and I'm trying to write one."

"Oh, how marvellous!" Mrs Thompson declared with exuberance.

Clarke looked at the daughter, who surprised him with a gentle, almost imperceptible smile. A secret smile. A Mona Lisa smile, as if she were trying to communicate her understanding of the contempt Clarke felt for her mother.

"More wine, Liz?" Breige called from the other side of the kitchen, making him jump.

"YES PLEASE, MRS McCULLOUGH," the Thompson girl replied in one of the shrillest and most grating voices that Clarke had ever heard. It was a voice so at odds with her appearance that Clarke felt cheated by his own preconceptions, and immediately decided that she wasn't the girl for him after all. Her smile was just a smile. It had no other language, no understanding and no hidden meaning.

A vision of Jane Etherington came to him bringing with it the taste of her warm kisses and the scent of her skin. A storm in a 'C' cup. Distracted for a moment, he felt empowered to stand up.

"Please excuse me... *Toilet*," Clarke hissed, invoking the most transparent of excuses, but escaping the thrall of the Thompsons. As he left the kitchen, he noticed that Ned was missing.

Despite the effects of the drink, Clarke easily found his way to the downstairs loo. First left at the front door, he remembered through the haze. He was careful, not wanting to stumble across Jake's coffin in the dark.

Clarke turned the knob of the toilet door and started to walk in, but stopped, gasped and shut it again when he discovered a groping couple writhing over the sink, tongue wrestling, hands everywhere, and whom, when he untangled them in his head, he recognised as Ned Labinski and Sinéad McCullough. Clarke stood outside in the hall, struggling to recover his bearings.

"What the hell?" he mumbled in disbelief.

A moment or two later, Clarke lolloped back towards the kitchen in a daze. He was about to re-enter when he stopped, deciding that he couldn't face any more of that either, and turned to retrace his steps down the hall. At the far end, by the front door, he noticed his bag still lying below the black-and-white photo of a teenage

Jake McCullough resplendent in a Derry Gaelic shirt. Clarke lifted his bag, opened the front door and wandered off into the drizzle.

23.

"The idiot's probably heading back to Belfast!"

"Then take my car and go after him, Ned. He's emotional. We all are."

"I can't drive, Breige. I've been drinking."

"Ned, this is an emergency... this is hardly the London rush hour," Breige said, raising her hands to encourage urgency.

"Are you sure?"

"Go on... get out of here..," she commanded, busying Ned towards the back door. "Go on. Go and get him, Ned!" she cried after him into the rain, steam rising on her cold breath.

What a plonker, Ned thought. This wasn't a good time for Charlie Clarke to go absent without leave.

Ned drove at a steady thirty until he reached the junction with the main carriageway in case anyone was following his progress from the kitchen window. But as soon as he turned onto the Belfast Road, and felt sure he was out of sight, he put his foot to the floor, pushing the car up to seventy and then eighty miles per hour. There was little or no traffic and the road was straight.

Ned hoped his hunch that Clarke would go straight back to the airport was right. He was too tired to be driving up and down to Belfast all night. But since Clarke's bag had vanished with him, it was the only conclusion to draw. It was also very easy to hitch a lift almost anywhere in Northern Ireland.

Ned could make out the houses dotted along the roadside and could see across the surrounding fields in the moonlight. It was light enough to spot Clarke should he be wandering along the road.

However, within forty-five minutes, Ned was approaching the final straight to Belfast City Airport. It had seemed to take a long time to get there even though he had been driving flat out the whole way. He felt guilty driving Breige's Laguna at top speed when she probably nursed it along at no more than thirty.

As Ned sped through the last twists and turns of the airport drive, which were supposed to be negotiated at ten miles per hour, he became aware of an eerie lack of traffic. And as the solitary terminal building came into view, he became aware of an eerier lack of travellers.

Just before the entrance, Ned pulled into the short-term car park, fumbling at the machine to retrieve his parking ticket and negotiate the barrier. He parked as close as he could to the terminal, yanking on the handbrake and struggling out of the door. He slammed the door, which got tangled with the seat belt, causing a heart-stopping delay and much frantic fiddling.

Ned sprinted across the car park, through the main entrance and the first security check, wondering why his erratic behaviour wasn't attracting more attention from the staff.

Running wasn't Ned's forte. It irritated him to discover that since the last time he had had to run anywhere (which he couldn't remember), his flesh had developed the tendency to bounce up and down with every stride, from the jowls on his face, to his chest, stomach and waist. Now everything seemed to wobble.

The airport terminal was quiet, but not deserted. Relieved, Ned soon came across ground staff and cabin crew and small crowds of people huddled in sleepy family groups waiting for the departures of the late-night charters to Tenerife and Corfu. Whenever he made eye contact, he offered a smile to reassure the recipient that he was a man in a hurry and not a rampaging madman.

Ned knew that Clarke would have been hard-pressed to catch the last flight to London. It was ten-thirty and the last flight would have taken off an hour before. He jogged through ticket sales and check-in, up the escalator through the shopping precinct, past the bar, cafeteria and buffet area, scanning from side to side, confident that if Clarke were there, he would spot his tall, gangly frame.

Ned had nearly run past him when he saw him. Clarke was sitting in the no-man's-land of plastic seating between the cafeteria and 'Departures'. He looked dejected; slouching and staring into space.

"Jesus Christ, Charlie! What the fuck are you doing?"

Clarke ignored him.

Ned stood speechless for a moment, gasping for air.

The silence was long and awkward.

"I'm not going."

"Where?"

"I'm not going to the funeral, Ned. I'm not going tomorrow."

"Why the hell– "

"I'm just too pissed off with the bastard right now."

"What do you mean? Like... I know he wasn't perfect."

"Wasn't perfect? Jesus, Ned. You should hear yourself."

"Hang on, Charlie... I really don't know where this is heading. I told you... You can forget anything Loulou McCall says. Anything she says is just fly-away balloons. Anyway Charlie, I don't know if I want to go over all this again."

"Well, exactly. That's why I'm going home, Ned. So you won't have to hear any more about it. I'm leaving you to it, mate."

Ned sighed before slumping down beside Clarke on the cheap plastic seats. The seats interlocked, joining at the hip like Siamese twins. Clarke produced a packet of battered Marlboro Lights, which he waved in Ned's direction, his trembling hands causing the fags to rattle around the pack.

They both lit up and drew deep breaths.

"I don't smoke, you know," Ned said, taking a long drag. "I gave up two Christmases ago," he continued in a gentle voice, almost a whisper. "But you never really give up, do you? You always think you've got it beaten but then sometime... any time... you'll be out drinking or at a party, and bingo! The temptation is there. You didn't realise before, but the addiction was there all the time, laughing at you for thinking that the power's with you because you've stopped... because you think you've given up... because you think you've got it beaten... but you haven't... it's still there... just waiting to catch you out in a weak moment like– "

"Ned... Did you know what he was up to?"

Another pause came punctuated with long drags and lugubrious plumes of tobacco smoke.

"Look, Charlie, I don't know exactly what you've been told, or by whom, but it doesn't really tally with what I know. Look, I loved the guy. I really loved the guy... warts and all... And did I know what he was like? I don't know. I hardly know myself. To me the guy was a joke. A big fucking joke. One of the funniest. One of the funniest jokes I've ever heard and will never get tired of hearing. A beautiful, simple joke. But take any joke and analyse it too closely and what have you got? A short story without a punchline. You're taking him too seriously. He might have been antisocial at times– "

"Alcoholic."

"Yes... probably... and Christ knows what Catherine had to put up with, but Jesus, Charlie... he could be very funny, you know. God, he could make me laugh. And did I know what he was up to? Yes, certainly. And did I disapprove? No... because I'm not as judgmental as some. But I'll tell you what, though, *he* didn't approve. He made himself thoroughly miserable at times... But me, yeah, I loved the guy. There was more fun in one of his smiles than most people have in a lifetime. There was more humanity in him than in anyone I've ever met... than maybe I'll ever meet. Being with him was so bloody entertaining. And then again, the guy was so bloody immature... unbelievably immature... Maybe that's why he had so much trouble with relationships. But that's what made him different... God, he never grew up. You know, in a nice way... like he was forever fifteen. He had the optimism of a fifteen-year-old. And he always thought he would turn a corner, that things would pick up. He always thought that somehow – and God knows how – things would even turn out right for him and Catherine. He *was* a dreamer."

"But– "

"No. Look, Charlie... No 'buts'. He just did the best he could. He had an image of what he wanted to be, God knows where it came from, and he had trouble living up to it. I think he always thought he should be leading some kind of very settled, suburban life, of car washing on Saturdays, traditional roast on Sundays and all that shite, but he just couldn't do it. He couldn't live up to his own expectations. He hated the thought of failing. I think that's when he took up drinking... heavy drinking... to dull the pain... relieve the pressure. He loved his friends, you know, Charlie... He really loved us. He even loved you, Charlie. I know he loved you. He told me. It was just the other week. We were laughing about you."

"Oh, thanks very much," Clarke murmured.

Ned had said enough. He had run out of words and meaning and couldn't be bothered to defend Jake any more. He kind of knew he didn't have to. It was too late.

"That was a decent eulogy, Ned. You really were fond of him, weren't you?"

They sat for a while, finishing their cigarettes in silence. Ned recovered his willpower, and thinking better of what he was doing, threw the last two thirds of his away in disgust.

"There's something else, Charlie."

"What's that?" Clarke asked, whilst fiddling with his fag.

Ned took a deep breath. *"The truth."*

"What?"

"The truth."

"What's that, Ned?"

"The truth about Jake."

"Oh, God. What now?"

Clarke braced himself for more discomfort.

"I'm going to tell you, but I don't think you deserve to know. Well, *you* do... but what I mean is that no one really deserves to know this... Not even you... our friend."

"What do you mean, *our friend?*"

"You see, Charlie, Jake was very confident, a very assertive and proud man. He felt comfortable with his macho image... the women, the partying and all that... as well as the home life bit... but... and it's a big *but*... it was a lie."

"What do you mean?"

"Er... How can I put this– "

"What?"

"OK Charlie... Jake was gay."

"*Gay?*"

"Yes."

"No way..."

Clarke was dumbstruck. After the chaos of the last week, however, nothing could surprise him now. He sat contemplating his shoes for a while. They needed re-heeling.

"Are you sure, Ned?"

"Sure."

"Oh? How do *you* know?" Clarke asked, trying to look into Ned's eyes to read his expression.

"*Because I am,*" Ned said, lowering his voice.

"Sure?"

"*Gay,*" Ned whispered, leaning closer.

Clarke glanced at his shoes again. A good clean might do for the funeral, he thought – forgetting that he wasn't going.

"Oh. I didn't know. Maybe I did... yeah, I had a clue... about you... not about him," Clarke mumbled, awkwardly.

"Actually, Charlie... I don't know how you're going to take this but... Jake and I were... were... Oh, you know– "

"An item?"

"Well, yeah. We were, actually."

"You – and Jake?"

Clarke swung round in his chair in disbelief and laughed.

"You and Jake were– "

"Lovers... I'm sorry I didn't tell you before, but– "

"*...he didn't want anyone to know..*," Clarke interrupted. "The stupid bastard. What about earlier... like when we were at college?"

"I don't know, Charlie. We were good friends... nothing more."

"What? You didn't even have an inkling? So what happened?"

"I don't think Jake really accepted that he was gay until he was older. I don't think he could face it until then. I don't think he wanted to be gay at all really. I don't think it suited his self-image to be... whatever century he gleaned that from. I think he had been suppressing it for years. I think he felt safer being straight, or pretending to be. To be quite honest, I think he preferred being straight. He liked running around with women and he loved being married. I think he loved the lifestyle, but – and it's another big but – it wasn't really him. He was gay, for Christ's sake. And there came a time when it really started to eat away at him and he got pretty screwed up about the whole thing. Not that you would notice."

"And when was this... I mean when did the problems begin?"

"About two or three years ago. Not long before *we* kind of got it together, actually. He needed to be with someone who understood him then. Someone who understood what he was going through."

"Right, OK. So that explains him, but what about you?"

"Well, fortunately, and it was fortunate, I hadn't seen Jake for a while. Not since he'd moved down to the West Country. I met him again in London after he'd moved back. He seemed so different. It was like meeting a stranger. He was so much less self-assured. It was like he was in shock, like he was sleepwalking. He appeared very vulnerable, he was drinking a lot... very unhappy... and he kind of looked like he needed someone... I had never really seen him *need* anybody like that before. It made him much more attractive as a person. More human. Less of a cartoon character."

"What about Catherine? Does she know?"

"That's been difficult. Jake would never talk about it. Even when she tried to confront him with the issue, I don't think he would, or could, discuss it... but she knows. Obviously, it's very difficult for her. Look, Charlie, she loved Jake. Still does – though I don't think she loves him in the same way as before. But she still loves him. She knew he was tortured – the whole thing was torturing her as well.

She loved him and wanted him to be happy. He was happy with me. I think she slowly grew to accept the way things were. I think we kind of became allies... allies in handling Jake. We get on... we're like family... What does it matter if she knew or didn't know the details? OK, so it's not what she would have wanted. Let's face it, an affair isn't a very good idea... but it's like a death... it's something you can learn to live with. Maybe it's different for the wife if the mistress is a man."

"So what happened? Why did it all fall apart? Why did he do whatever he did?" Clarke asked, taking a last drag on his cigarette.

"Why did he kill himself? Maybe he didn't really mean to... Obviously, this is a desperately difficult question for me to answer. God, I don't know... Maybe he was just fed up trying to live up to his expectations? Guilt maybe? I really don't know. I don't think he ever reconciled himself to being gay. He was pretty down when we met up again in London. Maybe I just helped postpone the inevitable."

"Was it inevitable? I have to say it's hard to pity him. Jesus, out of all of us you'd think I was the one that had more cause to do something like that. Look what I've been through, for Christ's sake!"

"You have a point– "

"Damn right, I do, Ned."

"But he was sick. It seems he suffered from depression."

"...And I just suffered. I guess that's the annoying thing about the sick. I mean, when they don't reach out and ask for help. Too much effing pride. Arrogant sod."

"Yeah, he was at times... Maybe he was afraid."

"Anyway... How are *you* coping?"

"Oh, ask me in a couple of months' time, Charlie. I mean, I'd walk barefoot on broken glass to bring him back, but it wouldn't change things. He'd only do it again. I think he was always going to. I think he was that curious."

"So why *did* Catherine send me off on a wild goose chase?"

"What? The eulogy thing? I don't know that she did send you on a wild-goose chase. You've found out everything, haven't you? She wanted you to know. You were his friend and you deserved to know. You're sensitive. She trusts you. And anyway, she genuinely wants someone to say something eloquent about Jake. A tribute. She knew you wouldn't disgrace him in church when you found out. She knows you're not judgmental... but *I'm* starting to wonder."

"Why didn't you just tell me, for fuck's sake?"

"Come on, Charlie, things have been difficult. It's doubly difficult if you are protecting a guy's memory. Jake has children, for God's sake... Anyway, you're her litmus paper. Catherine needed someone to test the colour of opinion. And that's you. She knows she is going to have to answer a lot of questions over the next few days. She wants to be prepared for whatever the funeral might bring. She has her dignity. And if your eulogy is an honest and fitting epitaph, it gives her a form of words to repeat *ad nauseam*. Hopefully, no one will give her a hard time."

Clarke thought for a moment.

"OK, but what about Jane Etherington?"

"What about her?"

"What was their relationship?"

"It was a good one. Like me, she was someone he met when he came back to London. He went out with her a lot, clubbing and stuff. They clicked. They got on. It was that simple."

"And did they– "

"*Have sex?* Well, I don't know about when they first met... I doubt it. He was coming out of the closet then – I don't think he would have climbed back in for her. Though you can never be sure with Jake."

"Oh. And what about you and Sinéad?"

"What do you mean?"

"You and Sinéad... I saw you two having a grapple in the loo."

"Oh Jesus, you saw that? Oh God, that was nothing... she was absolutely plastered. She followed me in there. I practically had to fight her off. You saw that? God, how embarrassing."

Clarke chuckled.

"I always hoped it was me she fancied."

"Actually, she does," Ned whispered.

"Oh, come on."

"She does. She told me. But she said you always look so bloody scared, and never seem interested or available."

"Well, *you're* obviously not..."

"Don't stereotype me. I could be tempted for all you know," Ned said, his smile returning.

They sat in silence for a while.

"Jesus, Ned. You must be heartbroken."

"It hasn't been easy. Maybe I could have done more to help him. But what? I loved him. What more can you do? At least it's over for Jake. He'd prefer to go out with a bang than a whimper. And Catherine *has* been very good. It's going to be bloody difficult for her, especially with the kids. But somehow we'll scrape through. She's an amazing woman, Charlie... Really amazing."

"Bloody hell, Ned. You're full of surprises."

"Yeah, well... Anyway... will you go tomorrow, Charlie?"

Clarke paused, sighed and then shook his head.

"Look, Ned. I'm sorry– "

"Oh, come– "

"No, Ned. I'm not going to be a hypocrite. I'm not going to go to the funeral and spout a load of garbage just to keep a bunch of people I've never met before, and another bunch of people I barely know, happy. I've had enough. I just want to go back to my boring life in London. I've had enough trauma to last a lifetime. If that idiot wanted to do away with himself, I don't see why I should get dragged into his shit."

"Well, I'd ask you to do it for Catherine... Breige... me... all of us."

"The answer's 'no', Ned."

"Why don't you sleep on it? I'll take you back to Breige's. The do-gooders will have gone by now. We'll have a few beers and then you can make your mind up in the morning. Jesus, you can't get too far tonight anyway, can you?"

"Look, Ned, I'll be fine right here. I'm not going. No."

"Jesus, Clarkey. You know you really can be hard work, sometimes."

152

"Yeah, probably, but at least I'm honest."

Ned gave a half-hearted wave and then turned to leave, disappointed to be making the long trip back on his own, but aware that Clarke was right.

24.

Sleep eluded Clarke. The chairs were too uncomfortable – hard with solid ridges moulded for the average backside – and the cloth stank of stale cigarette smoke. The random announcement *bing-bongs* from the airport tannoy also woke him anytime he thought he might be about to drop off. Clarke was resigned to a restless night.

"Hello, Mr Clarke."

Clarke hadn't expected company.

"Jesus, Funk! What the hell are you doing here?"

"Collecting my baggage. What's your excuse? You don't look so comfortable down there."

"There's been a change of plan."

"Oh?"

Funk, much to Clarke's annoyance, sat down. Bowing to the inevitable, Clarke swung his legs off the seating and swivelled himself upright, yawned and stretched. Funk, too, he noticed, looked tired.

"Baggage?"

"Yeah... It took an unscheduled detour from Heathrow to Glasgow. It's coming in on the last flight. It's due in in about half an hour, please God."

"It hasn't been your day, has it?"

"So far... No. Anyway... How about you? Don't tell me they've cancelled the funeral? You're not going, I take it?"

"Nope."

Clarke found his Marlboro Lights and jiggled them at Erroll Funk, who shook his head. Clarke lit up.

"I suppose you're going to give me a lecture on why I should go."

"Am I?"

"Why not? You'd be in good company."

"Look, man. I'm just sitting here waiting for my luggage. I can go and sit somewhere else if it'll make you feel better. But I wonder about that."

"About what?"

"What'll make you feel better."

"Yeah, well– "

"Look, Mr Clarke, what *is* your problem? You don't talk much."

"What do you mean?"

"I mean, you probably say plenty, but that's something else... I mean... do you ever really talk?"

"You're losing me."

"Your feelings. You're not very good at expressing your feelings."

"What's it to you?"

"Maybe I can help."

"How?"

"Maybe I understand."

Clarke shifted uneasily. He took a long drag on his cigarette, then leaned forwards to rest his arms on his knees.

"Mr Clarke, your friend is dead and you're beating yourself up about it. I wonder about that. Is it because you don't feel any remorse? Or maybe you think you could have done something... maybe you think you're a little to blame, right?"

"How the hell would you know?"

"Because I've been there."

"So?"

"So, it's natural. You're in shock, man."

"Oh, am I?"

"OK, so why aren't you going to the poor man's funeral?"

"Anger."

"Why 'anger'?"

"The bastard let us down."

"Obviously."

"Well?"

"Forgive him."

Clarke stood up and wandered off to the ATM on the far side of the concourse. He shook his head a lot. Funk leaned back in his seat and followed Clarke's progress.

"I can't forgive him," Clarke protested on his return. "There comes a cut-off point. There's stuff you can find out about someone that'll change your whole attitude towards them for good. It's a trust thing. A loyalty thing. I didn't know him. He sold me a lie."

"Forgive him."

"Easy to say."

"Maybe... Hey, I'm thirsty. Fancy a drink, Mr Clarke?"

Funk stood up.

The small airport bar, like the terminal building, was relatively new, but had been designed to look old and well-used. A theme bar. French. Cream walls with burgundy fittings. A French theme bar which sold only New World wine in miniature bottles, American lager and Irish stout. It was closing. The shutters had been pulled down except where the bar counter was raised to allow the late shift to carry the empties through to the back. Funk managed to wangle a couple of beers.

"You know, bearing a grudge is a heavy burden."

"Jesus, Funk, would you ever give up?"

"Well?"

"*A heavy burden?*" Clarke repeated.

"It's bad for your health... And you look like you've got enough on your plate."

"You seem to know a lot about me, Funk."

"As I say... it's written all over your face."

Clarke reached for a cigarette. Funk eyed him disapprovingly.

"Why don't you talk, man? Try. It's easy once you start," Funk continued.

"There are some things that are just too awful to put into words."

"Oh, I see. It's not 'anger'... it's 'fear'."

"Maybe."

"Ghosts?"

"Maybe."

"Your kids?"

"What the hell do you know about that?"

"I heard you, man."

"You heard *what?*"

"You... Talking in your sleep... on the plane. Calling out names... Alex and– "

"Please... Please... I don't want to go there."

"Look, *I'm* sorry."

"It's OK. Forget it."

Words left them. They got busy with their beers, taking small sips and picking at the paper labels with their nails.

Half a bottle later Clarke reached into a breast pocket and produced his wallet, flipped it open and pulled out a yellowing cutting with the headline: '*Drug addict kills two in Finchley*'. He passed it to Funk, who read it in silence.

"Do you understand, now?" Clarke asked quietly.

"Yes... I'm very sorry."

"It's not your fault. It's nobody's fault."

Another silence. Another sip or two.

"Is that why you're angry with your friend, Mr Clarke?"

"Maybe. He should have known better. He shouldn't have wasted his life."

"OK. But it's done. Where are you going to go from here?"

"I don't know. It's all very confusing."

"Do you blame yourself for what happened to your kids?"

"Of course. Survival guilt. Any parent would."

"Sure. But you couldn't have done anything."

"That's just it. I found out something about myself that afternoon which I despise and can't reconcile."

"What?"

"Look... well... it's the kid. The kid that did it. Well... how do I put this..? You see... when I came into the room, he was standing there... standing over them. He had a baseball bat in his hands... blood everywhere. He'd just battered my wife and kids to get at a pile of loose change, and what do I do? Nothing. No, worse... I put out my hand and he passes me the baseball bat. And then... and I can hardly believe this... I say 'thank you' and then I let him run off. I mean... he's just bludgeoned the life out of my kids and I say 'thank you'."

"You were stunned, man. In shock."

"Yes. But I should have killed him."

"No..."

"Yes! I should have beaten the fucking daylights out of him. But, you see, that's just it... this is what bugs me... I now know that if I'd been in a position to save them, I wouldn't have had the courage to do it. In that split second I would have backed off. I'm too fucking passive... too fucking polite... too bloody bourgeois... And now I haven't even got the drive to avenge them. I'm not man enough to do something truly brutal. I'm not man enough– "

"That's crap. You're letting him get to you. You're letting him win. Survive! Have the goddamn courage to survive. Do it for your kids. You're being too hard on yourself. It's not your fault!"

"I'm their father. They were at home. I failed to protect them."

"There was nothing you could do. Nothing."

"Oh, I don't know... I just don't know."

Clarke finished his beer.

"So this is why you're mad at your friend."

"Absolutely. He rubbed my nose in it. I hadn't seen him for years. We were just getting re-acquainted. I needed him. I was enjoying his company and then he goes and does that!"

"Look, you've got to talk to someone. Get help."

"No."

"Well, you've got to do something. You can't go on feeling sorry for yourself. It's a downward spiral. Get up, man... It's not all nettles... There's flowers out there, too."

"Maybe so... but it's not easy. I know where I want to be, it's just getting there. At the moment I'm stranded in the past. In that day. I can't move on."

"Look, man, can't you see it's just your imagination playing games with you? Every day's a new jigsaw. You've got today's pieces, but you're trying to make yesterday's puzzle... over and over again. That picture's not going to come, man! Don't do it! The pieces can't fit that way. That way lies madness. Don't go there, brother! Your friends can't afford to lose you, too. Stop being so hard on yourself. You're OK, you know. You're here... you're alive. Move on. Take the risk. Seems to me like you've got a phobia for living. Get over it. At least you've got a chance. And one other thing."

"What?"

"GO!" Funk said, raising his voice.

"Go?"

"To the funeral, man."

"Look, if you're so concerned about the bloody funeral, why don't you go?"

Erroll Funk stood up, shrugged and walked off to the baggage desk.

25.

Conversation fell flat in Breige's kitchen once Ned had left to look for Clarke. Eyes focused on infinity, visualising Ned's route while following the joins in the floor tiles or the grain on the table; the only sound, the glug of drink being poured and the coarse breathing of the smokers.

"Give us a song, Patsie!" Breige urged, to change the mood.

"*When I get home I'll tell my mum..,*" she warbled in a strangulated mock-Belfast vibrato. The song was taken up by the other women, also aware of the party's unspoken purpose: to preoccupy Catherine.

Catherine had found it easy to let herself be drawn into the pace of events. Drinking in the kitchen and joining in the drunken banter were mindless preoccupations that offered an escape from the blackness of thinking about Jake. It was only when one of the guests lowered their voice or touched her tenderly on the arm that she was reminded of her grief. Each well-intentioned smile or small act of sympathy was like a prick with a sharp knife. *I'm not a fucking sausage*, she thought. *I won't burst open. I'm not a boil that needs lancing.*

Her concern for her children didn't allow her the luxury of self-pity. But then someone would say, 'I'm so sorry!' or 'I know how you must be feeling!' and the temptation to scream 'You're not!' and 'You don't! How the hell would you know what I'm feeling?' burned to the bone.

Catherine liked Breige. Breige was rude to her. She employed a gallows humour that showed no fear of embarrassment.

"For God's sake, Catherine, lighten up and have another vodka, and get me one whilst you're at it," was all she need say.

It was only at bedtime and finally alone, that Catherine came out of character. Then the tears flowed and the bitterness surfaced. Bitter for the years she had wasted on Jake, for her lost career, for the sacrifice of her talent as a designer, for her children's loss of a father and the waste of her good looks. And then there would be little sleep. The dark night enveloping her, falling on her like a heavy black pillow – suffocating. Her breathing would accelerate. A panic attack. She would lie anticipating the dawn crawling imperceptibly towards the ever-dark night – and still it wouldn't come. Sleep: a rare fruit that couldn't be picked, a cruel joke which couldn't be shared.

And then she would wake, not knowing how long or if she had really slept at all, and with the morning would come a little more reason – a little less chaos. The reality of her grief a constant companion, but in the daylight less frightening – more containable. And through the day a harvesting of petty distractions, a fool's paradise of near normality and stark reminders, of a few good friends and a besieging army of foolish well-wishers.

And then the lonely night again, arriving too soon in late autumn. And if sleep came, it came with dreams – terrifying dreams of loss, of unending searches, of steep climbs up unconquerable peaks and of pain and suffering.

Catherine sat in the toilet dabbing her eyes with toilet roll.

"Psst! Catherine... You in there? Ned's back!" Breige hissed.

A deep breath. Head thrust back; eyes to the ceiling.

"With Charlie?"

"No good. He wouldn't come... never mind... Hey, have you been peeling onions in there again?" Breige said, hugging Catherine warmly as she opened the door.

"Yeah... one or two. My makeup OK?"

"You look a million dollars, pet."

"Don't, Breige."

"OK, you look bloody awful... like a giant panda... They're too pissed to notice, anyway."

"And Ned?"

"Och, don't worry about him."

26.

Ned had expected to return from the airport to a quieter and more sober house, but found the party in full swing. Despite failing in his task, Breige and company hailed him the conquering hero, welcoming him with hugs and kisses and a torrent of wine. It was easy to follow their example and seek relief in the bottle.

The next morning Ned awoke to a thumping hangover. He let it rest for about ten minutes before trying it out standing up, which then proved his theory that hangovers never appear so bad when you are lying down. A cautious trip into Breige's kitchen reassured him that the headache was nothing that a couple of paracetamol and a pint of water couldn't soothe; this would see him through until he got a hair of the dog later in the morning. The kitchen clock disappointed him, though – it was already half past eleven.

A *High Noon* atmosphere pervaded the kitchen, ensuring a thoughtful silence which Ned found easy to comply with as he sat at the table in his pyjamas. He was nibbling on a piece of dry toast, trying to regain some perspective. Lost in thought, he stared out of the window, distracted by the swooping and soaring of a plastic bag as it boomeranged around the garden, fat with air. For a moment, it came to hover in front of the kitchen window, before being swept away over the treetops. An eccentric species, the feral plastic bag, Ned thought.

The room started to fill with Jake's relatives, there for the wake and to view the deceased. The entire McCullough clan was gathering around the kitchen table and disturbing Ned's breakfast. Soon, the house would be as busy as it must have been on the day before for the prayer vigil. By lunchtime the house would be brimming with friends and neighbours, expecting tea and sandwiches and then something a little stronger. Breige's preparations were like those made for a siege: great walls of sandwiches, towers of booze. How strange, he thought, that the nervous anticipation for the funeral was like the run-up to a christening or wedding. Ned was relieved when Catherine joined him at the table.

"We'll all go in and see Jake before things get too busy in here, Catherine," Breige said, gently.

"Of course," Catherine replied. She seemed so demure. *"Ned. Clothes. Now!"* she hissed into Ned's ear, noticing his pyjamas.

Ned got showered and dressed as best he could in the time available, not readily recognising the final package in the mirror. He didn't do 'smart', but had had no choice under the circumstances. He rushed downstairs to the kitchen, his downy legs tingling as the synthetic of his trousers generated the electrical charge of a lightning strike and his thick mop waving wildly with the static of a hurried brushing. He entered the kitchen just in time to join the family group, Catherine at their head, who were moving through to the lounge at the back of the house for the viewing.

"Weren't you going to wait for me?" a voice whispered into Ned's ear.

"Jesus, Clarkey!" Ned shouted, clasping his hands to his chest in shock. "I thought we'd got rid of you."

"Yeah, well... I left my soap bag in the hall. I can't go anywhere without my moisturiser."

"Oh, Charlie... Thank God you're here," Catherine said, grasping his hands.

"Where the– "

"Look Ned, I'm here, OK? Let's just get this over with," Clarke said, turning to follow the rest of the group out into the hall.

A panoramic view of the Sperrin Mountains dominated the lounge despite the presence of the coffin. The largest room of the house, it easily accommodated the group. Jake's coffin rested at chest height on pine trestles and lay open. The lid had been removed and put to one side at the far end of the room. The mourners' view into the coffin was obscured by the white satin lining bulging over the sides like untamed meringue.

The group looked to Catherine to take a lead.

"Actually, Breige, I'd like to be left alone with him for a while. If that's all right with you."

"Sure Cathy... I'll be in the kitchen. Come on. We'll get out of your way for a bit," Breige said, turning to leave the room and ushering out Jake's relatives.

"No. Please stay. I'll need your support," Catherine said, catching Charlie and Ned by the wrist as they went to leave with the others.

Having composed themselves for a moment, they inched their way over to the coffin in careful steps, nervous as to what ghoulish sight awaited them, prepared for the garish sweep of the undertaker's makeup brush.

They stopped, stooped, and with the timing of ballroom dancers in formation, craned their necks to look down into the deep well of the coffin. They gasped, they recoiled and stepped back in perfect synchronisation. Silent. Unbelieving, they stepped forward again for further confirmation.

"*Who the hell is that?*" Ned shrieked, breaking the deafening silence.

"Shut up, Ned!" Clarke snapped, dashing over to retrieve the coffin lid and staggering back with it as fast as he could – it was heavy. He slid it onto the coffin with clumsy hands so that it lay askew. And all this before another word could be spoken.

The three stood sentry over the coffin, with the pallid demeanour of ghosts and turning mechanically – one to the other – to gauge the consensus of reaction.

"But who the fuck is that?" Ned asked in a hoarse whisper.

"He's aged since I last saw him," Catherine said, almost inaudibly.

"But who the fuck is that?" Ned repeated.

"Look, Ned... we don't bloody know... all right..!" Clarke barked.

"This isn't one of Jake's stupid pranks, is it?"

"Don't be crass, Ned. Of course it isn't. We all saw him in the hospital," Catherine said, relieved to hear laughter return to her voice, even if it was manic. "Anyway, I identified the corpse, and he was certainly dead then," she added.

"So there's no chance– "

"No chance, Ned," Clarke and Catherine said in unison.

The three stood, stunned.

Suddenly, the lounge door was ajar.

"Jesus! Sinéad!"

"Won't you let me see him before you do that, Charlie?" she said to Clarke whose hands were still gripping the coffin lid.

"Christ, Sinéad what are you– "

"I want to see him."

Too late. She had brushed past Catherine and Ned, and was halfway across the room. Over the final few feet, she faltered, edging her way to the coffin in pigeon steps, hands outstretched. The others stood frozen, mouths agape. When she reached the coffin, Sinéad lowered her hands onto Albert Lewis' face. Her trembling fingers danced across the nose, eyes and lips and patted the hair.

"Well?" Catherine asked in a croaky voice.

Sinéad turned round, wiping her red and watery eyes.

"Well?"

"It's not him," she said, despondent.

"Obviously."

"I really wish I hadn't done that."

"What?"

"Touched him."

"Why?"

"He feels so old now and wrinkly. It's not like Jake at all. His skin was so soft to the touch... like velvet."

"But what about the way he looks... You know..."

"Oh, God! You don't want me to look at him, do you? Oh, God. I couldn't. I couldn't. Poor Jake!"

"Sinéad– "

Catherine moved to comfort her, but Sinéad dashed out of the room in a flood of tears.

"For Christ's sake, Catherine, don't let Breige or anybody else see him," Clarke said, as his thoughts turned to the mourners in the kitchen.

"How the hell am I going to do that, Charlie?"

"I don't bloody know. Put your foot down. Throw a tantrum. Go a little nuts. They're probably expecting you to break down and do something a bit freaky any time now. Anyway, you're the widow, for God's sake, you'll think of something. Whatever happens we mustn't let them see the body. This body."

"Why the hell not?" Ned demanded.

They stood in silence, staring into the walnut veneer, trying to conjure up a good reason.

"Because we've all suffered enough, that's why. We've all had enough fuss. And because it doesn't matter a damn anyway," Clarke asserted.

"I agree," Catherine said, smiling in Clarke's direction.

"But what about the funeral? What's the point?" Ned asked, sounding desperate.

"Because we all need one. It'll be cathartic. We don't really need Jake... It'll be like a memorial service... Nobody will know anyway."

"Shit. What about the undertaker?"

"Listen, Ned, if he had looked in the coffin properly, we'd have heard by now, I can assure you. And besides, he's no need to."

"Who tarted the old guy up?"

"Prepared the corpse? I don't know... the undertakers in Brighton?" Catherine suggested.

"Who opened the coffin here, then?"

"Jesus, I don't know, Ned. Stop worrying. They probably didn't pay too much attention. I'm sure one body's pretty much the same as another to them."

"I don't care how much attention they paid at this end, but by the time I'm finished with these, they're not getting another chance," Clarke said, tightening down the large brass screws attached to the sides of the box with as much force as he could muster. "Don't worry, Ned. Let's just get him buried," he added, wiping the sweat from his brow on his shirtsleeve.

"I agree; Jake would laugh his head off," Catherine said, smiling.

"And this bloke needs buried anyway. It's not his fault," Clarke added.

"Don't you think he'll be missed?"

"Look, if they were aware that he's missing, we'd have heard something by now."

"How do we know he's not some sort of criminal, a drugs baron?"

"You're being stupid, Ned. You saw his face – he looked kind and sweet and has lots of laughter lines. I wouldn't worry too much. He looks old enough to be dead. I doubt if he was murdered or anything. It's just a simple mix-up," Catherine said.

"Some mix-up," Ned grunted.

They slid back into a silence of not knowing, staring wide-eyed and thinking that after this nothing could surprise them.

All of a sudden the door swung open again.

"Jesus!" Catherine shrieked, as Breige's head popped round the door. "You had me jumping out of my skin!"

"I was just wondering if any of you would like a cup of tea. Mind you, I'm sure you'd much rather have a drop of something stronger."

"No... er... No thank you, Breige. Not right now," Catherine said, trying to appear calm. Calm, but bereaved.

"Right you be then. Just let me know if you need anything or whatnot," Breige said, returning to the kitchen.

They stood quietly, waiting for some incisive thought.

"Right. That's it. We continue as planned. Jake's dead. We'll give him the funeral he would have wanted, but it's this body we're burying tomorrow. Simple," Catherine asserted.

"Agreed," Clarke enthused.

"Well, if you insist..," Ned said, limply.

"WE DO!"

"Jesus! This is just typical of Jake. He couldn't even take dying seriously," Ned whined.

"Yes, you're both full of surprises, Ned," Clarke added with a cruel inflection that wiped the smile from Ned's face.

"It's OK, Ned. It's OK," Catherine soothed. "Everything's going to be OK."

27.

Clarke lay in bed staring at the ceiling. He was imagining the fine cracks to be rivers, following their flow and interactions – anything to avoid getting up and getting ready for the funeral. The cracks, like vapour trails, seemed distant and surreal.

The previous night Clarke had resisted the temptation of more drink in Breige's kitchen and gone to bed early. It was rare that he would ever go to bed sober and sleep had been difficult: haunted when it came, by the screams of his children – horrific sounds for which there was no volume control or 'off' button. His feet had become snared in the bedsheet and exposed to the cold as the duvet was tossed through 90 degrees of bad dreaming. His pyjamas were more off than on. The arrangement was uncomfortable, but bearable. It was easier to bask in the idleness of inertia and do nothing.

Before bed he had called Jane Etherington to sort out a dinner date for his return. He tried her mobile, but couldn't get a ring tone. Probably bust – another victim of the wet weather – he imagined. He tried her home number, and left a garbled message on the answerphone. His intention had been to purr in a suave 'sexy-guy' voice about how he missed her and had been thinking of her. However, on hearing the formality of her announcement and once cued by the bleep, he was overwhelmed with stage fright and delivered his message in a stilted monotone – long-winded claptrap about leaving an umbrella at her flat. He hated himself for being such a coward, and cursed that he had phoned at all.

Beyond his bedroom door, the sound of running water and shuffling feet implied the start of the day. Clarke tried composing a line or two for the funeral, wishing that he'd jotted down some of the ideas that had come to him over the last week. He was damned if he could remember any of them now and was getting panicky since the funeral was only a couple of hours away. He should at least try and scribble a few notes on a fag packet, he thought, but couldn't think of anything that he wanted to say and didn't know where to find the inspiration.

The research had been thorough, but in light of what he had learned in the process, he wished he hadn't bothered with it. He was even less enthusiastic now that he knew that the funeral was a sham. It would be easier, and more gratifying for the congregation, he thought, if he simply regurgitated the usual cliches. But what would Jake want? Jake had had a warped sense of humour. Surely he would prefer him to spill the beans and tell the whole story? Jake would love the theatre. Ned was right, Jake would rather go out with a bang than a whimper, regardless of the collateral damage. Enough of the torture; surrendering to the inevitable, Clarke flung off the sheets and struggled to his feet.

Downstairs, there was an air of jollity at odds with the business of the day. Jake's children were running amok as a result of being shut up in the house for so much of the past week and seemed oblivious to the solemnity of the occasion.

Clarke walked past the living room on his way to the kitchen, cringing when he pictured the stowaway in Jake's coffin. Somehow, and much to his relief, Catherine had been successful in preventing a public viewing of the corpse during the wake. It wasn't easy and had upset a good many people, but it was her privilege. Their secret, so far, was safe. But where the hell was Jake? Clarke wondered. He couldn't even be relied upon to turn up to his own funeral.

For the third time in as many days, Jake's relatives gathered in the kitchen. The mood turned more formal. Conversations were now conveyed in nods and whispers. An aunt began to recite the rosary: *Hail Mary full of grace the Lord is with thee...* The rest joined in the murmured prayer: *Blessed art thou among women and blessed is the fruit of thy womb, Jesus...* Clarke stood watching from the back of the room, imagining the Christ-child popping into the world from Mary's womb like a shiny red conker leaping out of a shell. The prayer was repeated, over and over. Clarke felt out of place and out of time – an outsider.

Magee the undertaker appeared and selected six uncles, touching each gently on the arm and then leading them off to the lounge. Soon, the men reappeared bearing the coffin, which, due to their differing heights, was higher at the front than the back and sloping from left to right. They worked carefully, trying to walk in tandem as they guided the coffin through the narrow hall. The sight of the middle-aged men carrying their nephew's coffin had a sobering effect on the family. There was a gasp and the faint sound of crying. The uncles staggered towards the front door with the enthusiasm of first-time parachutists.

As the door opened Clarke had to shade his eyes from the sun, which at midday in autumn sat low on the horizon. The streets were dry – a novel sight accentuated by silence and, notably, the absence of the drumming of rain on tarmac.

Through the door, Clarke could see the townspeople of Clove Rock standing along the drive, a thick black carpet; a scene reminiscent of *Ryan's Daughter*.

Magee, the master of ceremonies, walked forward with the bearing of one who knows how to run a good funeral. Swinging round to face the house he prepared to receive the coffin as it emerged, its brass handles blinking sunlight. Jake's uncles bore the weight with grim determination, but a natural skill. Funerals, Clarke guessed, must be a common feature of life in Derry.

Clarke couldn't help but wonder about the old boy in the box and the circumstances which had brought him to Clove Rock.

Looking round, he sought out and then exchanged a smile of encouragement with Catherine and then Ned – a shared smile, the knowing smile of conspirators.

Breige came through the door after the coffin, followed by Catherine, Jake's sisters, the children, Jake's brothers, Clarke, Ned and the aunts. With the major cast assembled behind Jake's coffin, there was a pause whilst Magee concluded his business in the house.

The friends from London, a group of about fifteen, were gathered at the far end of the garden. They looked noticeably older, balder or greyer than when Clarke had last seen them. They could be distinguished from the townspeople by their clothes: more flamboyant in colour and cut; and by their body language: a shy foreign tongue.

Magee reappeared and inspected the coffin bearers, adjusting their grip, locking an arm here or moving a hand there. The bearers shrugged the coffin into a more comfortable position, and then nodded to signal that they were ready for the walk to the chapel.

As the coffin moved off close behind the hearse, Magee dropped back to usher forward close friends and family. Clarke walked a row or two back, absorbed by the ritual.

Every ten yards or so, Magee tapped another six men on the shoulder to instruct them to take over the carrying. In this way, the coffin rolled forward on a continuous wave of hands, bobbing along like a leaf in a stream. Clarke noticed that Magee avoided eye contact with him when searching for fresh recruits. He guessed he had been sized up and rejected as being too tall for the job. A sense of disappointment stung Clarke when he realised that he wouldn't be able to carry his friend to the chapel. But then he had to remind himself again that the deceased was a stranger.

The peace and quiet offered by the procession was Clarke's last opportunity to compose something for the eulogy. Grasping at straws he decided to be spontaneous and to speak off the cuff. He had done it before and it had worked well, so why not now? But then he remembered that he had been drunk then and it was the lack of inhibition which had loosened his tongue. His patter had worked; everyone had appeared to laugh, but then they were drunk too. Anyway, there was a marked difference between after dinner speaking at a rugby club stag night and eulogising for a funeral.

About a mile from the chapel, the road passed the clothing factory that Jake's father had established in the '50s. Magee stopped the procession and after a moment or two of prayer, supervised the loading of the coffin into the hearse. The last part of the journey would be by car.

28.

Wedding-cake white, St Brigid's chapel was visible for miles along the Glenshane Pass, the main road from Belfast to Derry. The local congregation, the Catholic population of the town, provided enough painters and decorators, builders, electricians, plasterers and volunteer cleaners to guarantee an immaculate appearance for God's house in Clove Rock.

The car park in front of the chapel had been freshly coated in thick black tarmac, which in the bright sunlight looked like liquorice gone mad. The congregation parted to leave a small channel for the cortege to fill as it crossed the black sea.

When the procession halted, Donal Magee assumed centre stage once more, strutting barrel-chested into full view and demanding the congregation's attention with his granite demeanour. Magee beckoned the coffin forward and organised his own men to carry it the short distance into the chapel.

As the coffin was carried up the aisle, relatives, friends and townspeople filed through the narrow entrance porch with the steady flow of egg-timer sand. It was only when Clarke looked back down the aisle and across the pews that he became fully aware of the significance of the event. Try as he might to picture his role in the theatre of the funeral service as a small walk-on part, he couldn't escape the thought that he needed to make an exceptional speech. The church was packed for the homecoming of a prodigal son, and Clarke knew his responsibility was to lead the celebrations.

Despite the chill in the air, Clarke felt hot and nervous. In his hurry to get dressed, he had tied his tie too tightly so that his shirt collar chafed the back of his neck. The collar had been rubbing all morning, and now his neck was red and sore. Clarke kept pulling at his tie to relieve the irritation, but with little success. His shoes also pinched and were making his heels blister.

Charlie Clarke and Ned Labinski slipped into the second pew, sliding along the polished seats on their backsides until they were directly behind Catherine, who was sitting with the children and the rest of Jake's immediate family. Catherine turned and smiled at them, winking at Clarke to offer reassurance.

"You OK, Charlie?" Ned asked.

"No. Not really."

Clarke was still fretting about his speech when two priests marched in through the sacristy door beside the altar. They wore beatific smiles, a professional demeanour, and exuded godliness. Wafts of incense hung about them, forewarning serious worship.

The younger priest addressed the congregation with well-practiced words, welcoming visitors, especially those from London, and the mourners from other denominations.

Clarke scrutinised the priest's words, observing the attentiveness of the congregation. He was just wondering if he should try and mimic the style, as he raked his hair with nervous fingers, when Ned nudged him and nodded towards the lectern in front of the altar.

"It's time," Ned whispered.

"Christ, Ned. What do I say?"

"You'll be OK... Just wing it."

Clarke squeezed out from behind the pew and walked over to stand at the lectern, his imagination churning with ideas. He looked over at Jake's coffin, then stole a glance at the congregation. Many sat with heads bowed or eyes averted. Scanning the faces, he spotted Loulou McCall sitting halfway down the chapel, almost upright and listing no more than five degrees over her neighbour –

a miracle of self-control. She was easy to spot, being the only person in the chapel wearing sunglasses. She was trying to merge into her surroundings, but failing dismally. The sight of Loulou McCall made him uncomfortable. God knows what she would say or do if she took a notion, he thought; but then, as he had said to Ned in London, you can't stop anyone going to a funeral.

Even though she had given the impression that she wouldn't attend, he was glad to see her. She was precisely the kind of friend that Jake would have wanted there. 'So what if she makes a scene? So what if she offends someone?' he would have protested. She had been a good friend.

Clarke gazed at the floor for a few seconds to compose himself. David Bowie's *Life on Mars* came to mind: *It's a God-awful sad affair...* The pathos of which touched a nerve. *To the girl with the mousy hair...* But then he knew it was only the sentimentality of the words that seemed appropriate – they weren't relevant to the situation, they just provoked a relevant response. Sentimentality, he realised, was a poor substitute for genuine emotion. Then he wondered if maybe he was emotionless – a sociopath, incapable of genuine feeling, who had to create a response through association. Did he really find the words of a song sadder than the reality of his friend's death?

Staring at the floor and waiting, Clarke recalled a documentary on Adolf Hitler. Hitler would stand silent for two to three minutes before addressing a rally, toying with his audience's emotions. And whenever they grew nervous and wondered if maybe there was something amiss, he would wait a bit longer still. The crowd would grow more anxious... Maybe he was ill? Maybe he wouldn't be speaking? The listening would be intent... and then... bang! He would scream out in his high-pitched thunderclap of a voice – ranting in a shrill bark – the audience rapt. Terrible but effective.

Clarke looked down and across the black-and-white geometric chessboard tiles stretching away from his scruffy shoes towards the heart of the church, counting in elephants: *eighteen elephants, nineteen elephants, twenty elephants...*

And then he began.

Initially, he spoke with confidence, talking in a clear voice with a steady rhythm, but without the reverberating volume he wanted. He was too nervous. His short staccato breaths wouldn't allow it.

"I was Jake's friend, not his best friend, but a good friend. But maybe, in the end, not good enough. Maybe none of us were. But I want you to know... I want you to know – those of you who don't know me – that I was a good friend to Jake and that we were close for many years. And I want you to know that I was asked to say some words because I am supposed to be good at this. I am supposed to be good at public speaking. But look at me. Today I can't be... I can't do it because I don't know what to say. I'm feeling pretty speechless right now."

Clarke swallowed hard and surveyed his audience. They were still listening. He looked up to the eaves high above them, levelled his head to continue and found himself staring into the dark lenses of Loulou McCall's sunglasses.

He began to ad-lib. Pre-planning was abandoned. Chaos felt natural.

"Jake was a brilliant man. Brilliant but troubled. His brilliance brought him every trophy that a life could be judged by: attractive wife, beautiful children, successful work. Every trophy, that is, except 'satisfaction'. Jake was never satisfied. Never at peace. Though he enjoyed much, he was rarely happy. This of course was unfair to all of us who knew and loved him. Whilst we were happy with him, he was never happy with himself. He was troubled. Always wanted more. Always wanted to be better. His was an insatiable appetite for perfection. But now his search is over, he is gone. He has left us. In some ways, ultimately, he has failed us.

"But of course there was success. As a writer, he won awards for his children's books. He was mostly a good husband and a good father. He loved people and they took to him... He was a bon viveur, a raconteur, the life and soul of the party. But there was also the other side, the darker side of his personality that few of us knew.

"As it turns out, I realise that I didn't know Jake very well at all. Very few of us did. I know him a bit better now, I think. Now that

I have found out a little more about some of his problems. But – and it is a big but – it isn't for me, or anybody for that matter, to try and explain the essence of this man. He was too rare. Too special. Too brilliant.

"His was a unique scent – enchanting, exotic, intoxicating... the formula of which has been lost... lost on a wild and destructive wind. A wild whim. We are left with only the vaguest memory of its essence. We will remember it occasionally when faint hints of its spice return when we least expect. Haunting us. Tantalising us. Teasing us like childhood memories evoked by the smell of the sea or a certain flower. Moving us when we catch a hint of the essence, driving us to mourn the loss of childhood innocence.

"Catherine asked me to say a few words for Jake, but I can't really, and I won't. I am not lost for words. There are none."

Clarke froze. For the first time since the news of Jake's death, he was overcome with the emotion of loss. It confused him. He had lost so much in recent years, but had managed to maintain a cold detachment. Now, in front of three hundred strangers, he was overwhelmed, poleaxed by an almost unbearably sharp pain. His eyes were moist and his breathing was such that he knew that to continue would bring on tears; they were already welling in his eyes.

"I'm sorry... But it's OK to cry, you know..." Clarke struggled to get the words out. "We should do it more often."

Tears rolled down his cheeks, his chest heaved.

"Let's face it, tears are a better testament to the man than any words I could say... I guess they are a measure of my love... Maybe that's what tears are for... for endearment.

"But, silly man. He was one of the cleverest and funniest people I've ever met. The man had a fantastic brain, but finally it didn't help him a jot. It was a curse.

"Jake was a hell of a guy, but he wasn't a particularly good guy. Sure he was special, but he wasn't a saint. He was quite often an absolute sod, but, and it's another big but, he lived life like there was no tomorrow. There was an intensity about Jake that made it uncomfortable to stand near him at times. His heat was ferocious. White hot. And now, there is no tomorrow.

"Did any of us know him? Really know him? No way. No. Absolutely not. That was his beauty. His allure. An unknown soldier. We are all unknown soldiers."

Clarke sighed, unsure whether he should continue... go on in the vain hope that sooner or later he would hit on precisely the right thing to say. He didn't feel that he had quite finished yet, but then he wasn't sure if he had actually started either. It wasn't that he felt awkward or uncomfortable with what he was saying, but his moment had passed.

There was an uneasy silence in the chapel, made noisier by people shifting in their seats, shuffling their feet and coughing, made nervous by the combination of Clarke's outpourings and bad language.

Clarke turned towards the front row of the congregation and saw Ned grinning up at him. It took him by surprise. Clarke couldn't tell whether Ned was laughing at him or with him. He looked strangely at ease.

Clarke stood rooted to the spot, puzzled by Ned's curious smile. He looked across to check the congregation. They however, were still sitting with blank, mournful expressions.

Turning round, he noticed that the two priests, seated on the far side of the altar, had averted their eyes in embarrassment and were staring down at their feet, searching for their reflections in the gleaming polish of their shoes.

By the time Clarke looked back round, Ned was standing beside him, enveloping him in his long spindly arms and cushioning his head on his shoulder.

"It's OK, Charlie. You did fine. You did fine," Ned whispered.

"It was shite... but I don't care, you know? But maybe it's what he would have wanted – a bit of emotional turmoil; a bit of a cock-up; a tour de farce."

"Absolutely."

Ned released Clarke, and turned to address the congregation.

"Erm... I have something of a surprise," he said with quiet confidence. "It's something that Jake requested."

Ned stepped to his left and, turning his back on the congregation, lifted a purple drape which had been arranged over what appeared to be a wooden chest to one side of the coffin. Once removed, the drape revealed a large television monitor and video machine sitting on an industrial-looking trolley – the kind of ageing kit found in a polytechnic or school. Ned was blushing. *This isn't a good sign*, Clarke thought.

"I'm sorry," Ned whispered to Clarke. "It wasn't my idea."

Clarke shrugged and returned to his pew.

Ned was now fiddling with a package that he had pulled from a pocket in his overcoat. A small black box emerged through his fumbling fingers and a mass of crumpled brown postal paper. It was a video cassette.

"I received this tape in the post on Wednesday from Jake's solicitors," he said, addressing the congregation. "It appears that Jake had left instructions that it be played here today. Anyway, I won't explain further."

Ned switched on the TV and pushed the cassette home into the VCR. He pressed the 'play' button and stood back.

A hubbub of mumbling filled the church; heads turning, chattering with nervous excitement. Clarke caught Ned's attention as he was returning to sit beside him. Ned frowned. Clarke turned to look at Catherine. She was also frowning.

Meanwhile, a clock appeared on screen, counting down from twenty seconds to zero to cue the film. On 'zero' the screen dissolved to a wide-angle shot of a broad expanse of sea and the mouth of a river filmed from a high vantage point. It was a bright, sunny day and the heat haze in the near distance marred the clarity of the panoramic view, but the colour of the sea and of the beach around the spit were strong and intense – brilliant blue and yellow, even on video. The scene was bereft of people.

Clarke identified the Foyle estuary, the water that divides Northern Ireland from County Donegal in the Republic. The camera was on the Greencastle side of the estuary high up on the road to Kinnagoe Bay. Clarke recognised the tiny fishing harbour below and the view of Kealys, the seafood bar on the quay. The twin towns of Portrush and Portstewart, glinting in the far distance, confirmed it. He could also see Rathlin Island, a delicate brush stroke, and the hills of the Mull of Kintyre lying like slugs of toothpaste squeezed along the horizon. The cameraman had picked his day well, Clarke thought.

The camera pulled back to reveal the figure of a man with his back to the lens, bent over a little Edwardian coffee table and turning the handle of an old wind-up record player. He was dressed in a white suit, white shirt and white canvas shoes and was standing on a small rectangle of gravel. A viewing point. After forty or fifty vigorous cranks, the man stopped to lift the stylus and place it on the spinning disc.

A high-pitched scratching of metal on Bakelite preceded the brass of a swing orchestra and a piano playing a melody in a minor key. After a few bars, a woman's voice joined the fray, whose half-talking, half-singing sounded not too dissimilar to the scratching noise made by the needle. It wasn't until the intro led into the first verse that Clarke could detect that the song was Gershwin. Ira Gershwin.

He leant over to Ned...

"*The Man I Love?*" he whispered.

"Sophie Tucker..," Ned replied, nodding. "His favourite."

Meanwhile, the figure had turned around and was moving over to the stripy canvas deckchair beside the record player.

The camera zoomed in on Jake McCullough, posing in post-colonial style with what one would guess was a huge gin and tonic and a threatening-looking Havana – more curtain pole than cigar.

"*Hello and welcome to my funeral..,*" he beamed, flashing a gameshow-host smile. The congregation were now watching the screen in silence. Clarke turned to Ned, who shrugged.

"Why did he like to wear white?" Clarke whispered.

"He thought it made him look virginal... virginal and innocent."

"Pah!"

"I'm sorry to be so pretentious, but I guess this is my day... and like any spoilt child, I think I should be allowed to indulge myself a little. I do hope you don't mind. I thought, as well, that if I was going to appear at my own funeral, I would appear as I am... was... in my prime... so here I am, aged thirty... I've still got my own hair, and my own teeth... who knows what that guy in the box looks like?" Jake said, nodding towards the coffin beside the TV monitor.

"If only he knew," Ned whispered.
"How did he know which side to nod to?"
"Beginner's luck?"
"Typical."
Clarke glanced at Catherine, who wrinkled up her features in an *I-know-nothing-about-this* kind of face, and possibly, looking more amused than distressed.

"...Anyway, I just wanted to thank you all for being such good friends and for coming to my funeral," Jake continued on screen. *"Don't be sad for me... just think of me here... in this beautiful place... Donegal... Inishowen... my spiritual home."*

Looking emotional, Jake took a large sip of his G&T. It seemed that he was trying to stop himself from weeping and was a little bit tipsy. Not so drunk as to be incoherent or incapacitated, but heading that way.
A tear or two fell freely. He raised his hands with fingers splayed as if to say *enough, enough,* rolled his head from side to side to shake off the tears and regained his composure.

"I know I shouldn't really be here... er... there... in the chapel with you... God knows what the parish priest will say... but I want to reassure you all that being dead isn't so awful... I mean, look at me... gin and tonic, cigar (I've always wanted to smoke in church), my favourite music... my favourite place in Donegal... This is my little piece of Heaven, you know, and I'm really very happy here...

Oh, and if you're ever passing this way... think of me sitting here, enjoying the view... even when it's raining... And if you love Donegal, let's face it... you've got to like the rain."

Jake sat back, closing his eyes and letting the sun warm his face for a while, before sitting up abruptly and turning to the camera...

"I hope you're not there, Mother... but if for any reason you are, I would like to say sorry I've gone before you. Don't be distressed. You know I love you. I wasn't such a bad boy really, you know... My pleasures were hard won – my vices few."

Jake tilted his head back and took a large puff on his cigar, which, when released, created a kind of dry ice effect. He sat silently for a few moments, then mumbled some unintelligible curses which evolved into something like verse:

"I cried tonight;
Shattered like the night sky,
Shivering like the stars,
Alone like the moon.
And the memory fades,
Love, a sad ghost.
I say: 'I did not love her',
But I loved her,
Our time was so short,
The pain lasts so long...
Blah, blah, blah...'
That's it... C'est tout... The Grim Reaper beckons..."

Jake closed his eyes. Suspecting that this might be the end, the cameraman zoomed in. Jake's eyes opened, squinting in the sunlight.

"Oh... Goodbye and thank you."

The camera focused on Jake's drink-reddened face until it was obscured by the sun glaring into the lens. And then he was gone.

The chapel was silent. Clarke and Ned looked over to the two priests, who had dislodged themselves from their perches and were sweeping down to the front of the altar on feet made invisible beneath billowing cassocks. They reclaimed their vantage point at the top of the altar steps to wrest back control of the proceedings.

"And now we will sing the Quaker hymn *Lord of the Dance*. The Copland arrangement. Hymn number two hundred and four," the younger priest announced, in a hurry to move things along. He nodded up to the organ loft to indicate to the organist that he should commence with the first verse without delay, and then with a sweet smile turned back to face the pews, hoping that the act of hymn singing might dispel the open-mouthed incredulity that had overwhelmed the congregation, dumb since the end of Jake's bizarre tape.

At first, the honeyed tone of the chapel organ drowned out any efforts of the congregation to sing. The only sound seemed to be emanating from the cultured larynx of the young priest, who sang with the polish of an experienced performer:

"Dance then, whoever you may be..."

Eyes half closed, he imagined that he was a Quaker... a Quaker priest administering to a simple pioneer farming flock somewhere on a vast American prairie. He would wear a red gingham shirt over his dog collar and tan cowboy boots under his Levis. A Quaker cowboy priest.

By the end of the second or third line of the hymn, a murmuring could be heard breaking over the congregation like a cold sweat. The congregation's voice, as dry as biscuits, failed at first to match the enthusiasm of the young priest. But his energy was infectious and, building with each verse, the volume of the communal singing rose louder until the chapel was filled with sound. Here and there, smiles reappeared.

The older priest – the parish priest – wore an expression like thunder, enraged by the fiasco unfolding before him. A purist, he grieved for the passing of the Latin Mass. Without mouthing the words of the hymn, he opened and shut his mouth in time to the music like a guppy. He hated modernism and modern hymns – guitars and tambourines in particular. Never again would he concede to his young curate's request to have a video machine brought into the chapel. Never again would he concede to any of the curate's requests against his better judgement.

The silence left behind by the deep reverberations of the chapel organ on playing the last chord of the hymn left a vast space for the imagination to fill.

"May the peace of Christ ever dwell in your home. May the angels of God protect it, and may the Holy Family of Nazareth be its model and inspiration. Amen," the young priest chirped with enthusiasm as he half sang the concluding rite in a beautiful tenor, but in a sprint and drawing another grimace from the parish priest, who was unimpressed that, in the heat of the moment, his curate had recited the concluding rite from last Saturday's wedding instead of the sombre concluding rite for today's funeral.

The old priest, taking his cue, mumbo-jumbo'd through the final blessing, crossed himself extravagantly, spun round and marched off, his young curate struggling to keep pace. Facing the altar, they genuflected before the immense wooden crucifix sitting centred between two rows of tall silver candlesticks, and upon which Jesus' head seemed to hang lower than usual, eyes closed to the mayhem.

Donal Magee and his men approached Jake's coffin and lifted Albert shoulder-high to carry him out of the chapel for the committal in the graveyard. He would be laid to rest beside Jake's father, in the company of an eclectic mix of the late citizens of Clove Rock, from past priests to former IRA divisional commanders.

Clarke sighed. The ordeal was over. Nothing could ever be so tortuous again, he thought. He looked at Ned and slapped a hand on Ned's thigh to express his relief.

"He's mad," Ned whispered.

"Jake?"

"Who else?"

"Well, he was different all right. Anyway, let's get the bugger buried..."

As Clarke got to his feet, he fought to suppress a smile; relieved that their secret was about to be buried with Albert Lewis.

Up in the organ loft, the chapel's elderly organist was just about to thump out excerpts from Purcell's *Music for the Funeral of Queen Mary*, to accompany the mourners from the chapel – confident that the Republicans amongst them would be unaware of the Royalist connection – when he was rudely interrupted by a strange humming emanating from the back of the chapel. It was sinister and soft-sounding at first, like a low rumble, but rising in volume.

Looking into the shaving mirror gaffer-taped above the stops on the left-hand side of the organ, he caught a glimpse of a crowd of red-coated strangers. They were standing behind the last row of pews at the back of the chapel and swaying as they hummed.

Having practiced the Purcell all week for the McCullough funeral, the elderly organist was miffed at not being able to launch into the opening bars as planned for this precise moment. Stops pulled, and hands raised above the keyboard with fingers flexed, he teetered on the brink of going ahead regardless of the noise coming from the back of the chapel. He knew that there could be no competition for the booming bass pipes of the chapel organ, but theirs was a mysterious sound and his innate musicality made him curious and eager to hear more. The sound was also familiar. The more he heard, the more he liked, despite his pique.

The congregation were also looking perplexed as they got to their feet to follow the coffin out to the graveside. The sight of a gospel choir at the back of *their* church in central Northern Ireland, singing a gentle lament in a foreign tongue, was not one they were used to. They searched their orders of service for a reference. There was none.

"What the hell's this?" Ned whispered into Clarke's ear, as they led the congregation out of the church, close behind Jake's family.

"*Mwfanwy.*"

"What?"

"*Mwfanwy.* It's a Welsh lament. Listen... it's very beautiful."

"Oh, how appropriate," Ned said, with all the sarcasm he could muster. "And how the hell do you know what it is?"

"Because I'm morbid and I like morbid music, and because I know about music."

"And I suppose you know who those guys are?"

"Well, actually, I do. The tall guy at the front waving his arms is Erroll Funk III, and they're the Houston Seventh Day Tabernacle Gospel Choir."

"And what the hell are they doing here? I suppose you know that as well," Ned said, forgetting to whisper his profanities and drawing disapproving looks.

"Well, I mentioned to Erroll on the plane that I was going to a funeral and where it would be. You can't miss this place on the way through to Derry. It's a small tribute. Don't you think Jake would just love it? I can almost hear him laughing."

"But what are a bunch of American gospel singers doing singing *Mevanwee*, or whatever it's called?"

"*Mwfanwy*... I haven't got a clue– "

"Oh, that makes a change– "

"Unless they learnt it from the Treorchy Male Voice Choir."

"Of course they did, Charlie... of course they did... it all seems so obvious to me now."

Erroll Funk exchanged a warm handshake with Clarke in the graveyard.

"I didn't really mean for you to come, you know. I was being ironic," Clarke whispered

"I'm American, Mr Clarke. We don't do irony."

"It's good to see you, anyway. Thanks for coming."

Behind them the old priest completed the committal of Albert Lewis' body to Irish soil. The deep pit, collared with PVC sheeting, was already filling with a muddy ooze – a residue from the earlier rain. It would be hard, Clarke thought, for the old priest to find some loose earth to sprinkle.

EPILOGUE

Charlie Clarke sat in his studio bathed in sunlight. Fine dust particles were dancing about him in the glare like the wind-scattered heads of a dandelion clock. It was Monday morning again.

Clarke was transfixed by the dust and lost in a daydream – a half-sleep – in which he followed a long and winding train of thought that led further and further away from the grey reality of the day unfolding in South East London, and back to Jake's funeral in Clove Rock. The funeral seemed months ago.

It had taken less time than he had imagined to settle into his old routine and for a degree of normality to return to his life in the city. Only two weeks had elapsed since the funeral and already his memory of it was becoming sketchy. That he could slip back into his former pattern of life so easily irked him and did nothing to lessen the feeling of guilt that hung around him like a bad smell.

Why he still felt guilty after the funeral, he did not know. It wasn't the survivor guilt that he associated with the children's murder. This was a different feeling and it didn't make sense. He could understand, for instance, that he might feel guilty, because Jake's death and the events thereafter had brought excitement and direction to his rather dull life; that it had been an almost enjoyable experience at times, giving him a special purpose for a while, but he knew it wasn't this.

He had enjoyed being useful to Ned and Catherine – being part of the team. As one of the deceased's oldest friends, he had also enjoyed the sympathy that his grief had elicited from others. The funeral had given him status. Now, however, the old college friends and other acquaintances had faded into the background – not to be seen until the next funeral, wedding, christening or birth.

Staring into the dust for a little longer, he decided that maybe he felt deflated rather than guilty. Deflated after the excitement was over and the company gone, leaving him alone at the mercy of his demons and loathsome routine once more.

On his return to London, Clarke had had to work. Work hard. The backlog of unfinished jobs gave him no option. There were bills to be paid and an ex-wife to be supported. On the plane home, he had promised himself a fresh start. He wasn't filled with optimism and had little energy for new adventures, however. Jake's suicide had left him feeling vulnerable. Erroll Funk had been right, too; he must develop some new interests, and probably should seek help, some counselling.

Now, it was Monday morning again, and for all his good intentions he found himself struggling through the same routine he had left on the Friday two weeks before. Another mad dash in the London traffic, another pile of work, another long list of business contacts to phone, suppliers to pay, invoices to type, appointments to make, miss or break. He could feel himself sinking into a familiar rut.

For the moment, however, he sat staring glassy-eyed, paralysed by deep thought, delaying for a few moments the slide back into the torrent of a working life, the new agenda shelved.

As soon as the plane from Belfast had landed at Heathrow airport on the Tuesday morning following the funeral and once he had battled his away across London on the tube to the flat in Battersea, he had telephoned Jane Etherington.

Reluctant, but excited, he was as nervous as hell about making the call, and didn't like the feeling. It didn't bode well. If he couldn't phone her without becoming a bag of nerves, what hope was there? The anxiety revealed his insecurity. He comforted himself with the thought that maybe it was his vulnerability that had attracted her to him.

They arranged to rendezvous for a drink in the Groucho Club that night. It was less than a week since they had met there for the first time, but already it felt like a lifetime. In some respects, with the passing of Jake's funeral, it was.

The conversation was stilted. There were awkward pauses poorly filled. He went back to her place and stayed over, but regretted it. He felt uncomfortable, and disappointed that he couldn't relax, even when fortified with wine.

They slept together, but it was a self-serving intimacy that made them both feel self-conscious and unsatisfied. By the morning, he had decided that things shouldn't progress further. He wasn't ready for a relationship. Not with her. Not with anybody. Not then anyway. Not yet after the divorce. Jane Etherington's association with Jake didn't help either. It was easier not to get involved with her.

As soon as she was awake, he told her. He regretted the words almost as they were spoken, but knew it was for the best. He didn't deserve her. She felt rejected, but let him go without giving him too much grief. She wasn't in the mood for brooding. She didn't have time for disappointment.

Now, a week later, he sat in his studio staring at the dust and trying to diagnose the symptoms. Suddenly, as a cloud passed overhead and the dust stopped dancing, he could see what was troubling him. It wasn't guilt, but loneliness.

An acquired taste, loneliness was a bittersweet lifestyle he had grown accustomed to. It made him feel comfortable. He realised that he preferred to be comfortable and lonely rather than to risk discomfort for happiness. He clung to loneliness like an old friend, familiar and undemanding.

＊＊＊＊＊＊＊

Jake McCullough came into Clarke's thoughts every day for the first month or two after the funeral. But the suicide was becoming an uncomfortable memory he would rather let fade. Clarke had had enough of tears.

Through the winter and the onset of spring, he met up with Ned and Catherine on a regular basis. They were like a self-help group and got together at least once a week. It was a little good that had come out of a bad experience. Clarke liked to spend weekends visiting Catherine in her new house in Kew. She hadn't wanted to stay either in the Finchley house or in Finchley after Jake's death. There were too many ghosts.

Moving out to South West London had pleased her. It was greener. There were parks and the River Thames and excellent restaurants. People liked to visit her there. And there were good schools.

Clarke often stayed over at weekends, arriving in time to make dinner on the Saturday, and staying through to the Sunday evening.

At first, Clarke's motivation was to keep a fatherly eye on Catherine, as he felt Jake would want him to. Soon however, he came for her company and friendship. She was very gentle, and seemed to understand him. And he loved playing with the kids.

Ned would also drop by. Clarke and Ned were like her adopted children. An extended family. The drive home on the Sunday evening was hateful. It emphasised his loneliness and encouraged him to drink.

＊＊＊＊＊＊＊

It was about six months after Jake's funeral that Breige McCullough first noticed it happen. It was Donal Magee, the undertaker – he had

192

developed the habit of winking at her whenever their paths crossed about the town. It was wasn't a 'come on' – a wink that said 'How about it big girl?' – they were both too old for that kind of carry-on, she knew. Well, he certainly was, being nearly eighty, but then again men rarely, if ever, change. And the wink wasn't a nervous tic – it was too expressive. Blink and you would miss it, but it was sly and deliberate. And he did it every time they passed one another on the street or the supermarket aisles. Breige started to imagine that he knew something she didn't. That was it, she thought. *Yep, he's got one over on me and he's letting me know it.*

But then the winking stopped. Suddenly. And she couldn't work out why. She imagined it was either because she had never reacted to it or because, one day, he just plain forgot to do it at all, and then that was it – over.

It was Magee's wife who had put a stop to it. She caught him in the act. She had been queuing in the Post Office – an interminably long wait on giro day – and whilst staring back onto the street through the large shop window, saw Magee ambling down the pavement on the far side of Main Street. Thoughts of how smart he looked in his new two-piece and how she must get him to clean out the fish pond before the winter set in, vanished the moment she noticed his expression change when Breige McCullough stepped out of Bolans the Chemist and into his path. Concerned and now watching him like a hawk, Magee's wife spotted the wink. *She* certainly didn't think he was too old to be making passes at sixty-year-old widows. A week of silence and cold salads – mounds of lettuce swathed in sliced beetroot and grated carrot – put an end to the winking.

Breige soon forgot about Magee's odd behaviour. She was possessed of a positive mindset that didn't allow her to dwell. After Jake's death there were too many who depended on her strength and support. Her's was a big family.

Donal Magee never forgot Jake McCullough. He couldn't. He knew the secret. He had seen Albert Lewis lying in Jake's coffin.

No one else knew, but he felt the weight of the secret burning into him like a shard of shrapnel that couldn't be removed. He became obsessed by the mystery.

Magee wondered long and often where Jake might be. He hoped he was alive and well and had escaped to a better life. Every month he imagined Jake enjoying the exotic scene on the new page of the Co-op calendar hanging behind his desk. December looked good; maybe Jake was in Venezuela – turquoise sea and bright yellow sand.

When Jake's coffin had arrived off the ferry from Scotland, Magee decided that it would be he who would dress the corpse for the funeral. Jake was the nearest thing Clove Rock had to a celebrity and Magee was damned if anybody else at the firm was going to steal the limelight at the wake. It would be a last hurrah for Magee before his retirement and the handing over of the reins to his young nephews.

Magee's interest in doing a fine paint job on Jake McCullough was quickly supplanted by the surprise of finding Albert Lewis in the box. In forty years as an undertaker Magee had never seen the like. Forty years of routine had transformed a once tricky and skilful art into a regimented procedure. But like the bus driver who makes two or three unscheduled laps of a roundabout on their retirement day, Magee – normally an upright and conscientious servant to the community – thought he had earned the right to a little eccentricity and couldn't resist the opportunity of performing one small anarchic act. He painted Albert Lewis' face with all the skill and delicacy he could muster, then replaced the lid, smiling wickedly at the thought of the chaos at the wake to come.

But the chaos didn't come and neither then did an explanation. Never a word, nor a sign. And now Magee was in a quandary – stuck between not knowing the answer to the mystery and unable to pursue the matter because of his involvement. He was a conspirator without allies and unable to ask questions.

Since he saw Breige McCullough the most often of those he believed could provide an explanation, she became his prime target. But out of respect and for fear of exposure, he knew he could never broach the subject with her. *What if she knows nothing? She'll either denounce me or think I'm mad!* he thought. A well-timed wink however could speak volumes. She would recognise the sign, understand that he shared her secret and then confide in him. But then that smallest of lines of communication was cut off.

Magee was left without an answer to the riddle of Jake McCullough. Years of frustration, of curiosity and of staring at Co-op calendars drained him and when he did dare break his silence and raise the subject it was too late. He was too old. No one could or would hear him or was able to decipher his mad and mumbled ramblings.

It was the not knowing that finally killed him. Missing for two days, the old parish priest found him face-down in the graveyard behind the chapel, lying on top of what was left of Albert Lewis' bones; the effort of digging down to the coffin, the forcing open of the lid and the frustration of finding little in the box that offered a clue was more than his weakened heart could bear. No suspicion was aroused by the rusty medal found gripped in Magee's right hand.

* * * * * * * *

Within weeks of the funeral, Erroll Funk III became a convert. He embraced atheism. On waking one morning, something clicked in his brain and it suddenly occurred to him that religion – all religions – were bunk; his brand in particular.

He didn't find this disturbing. Funk felt exceedingly calm.

There was no relation between this dawning and his brief association with Charles Clarke – Funk's was a DIY conversion. And none of his friends or relatives were shocked or upset by the news, because Funk didn't tell them. Too many of those that he loved and whose respect he enjoyed, depended on him for spiritual guidance; he couldn't let them down and he wouldn't.

Funk continued to sing in the choir, to evangelise the Word and to attract new recruits to the club. It was his job. Also, he found that he enjoyed his religious activities more as an atheist. He no longer lived in fear of God. The more he embraced atheism, the easier he found it to convert others to Christ. He was less earnest in his patter, his eyes had lost their ferocious burn, he was warm and welcoming, his words were gentler. He became kind. He drew in waiverers and reassured the doubters. The fire and brimstone were quelled.

And never once did he feel guilty about his duplicity. He never once questioned the legitimacy of what he was doing. Like Clarke, he grew to love God like adults love Santa, and he knew that the Christian ethic was right. His new faith calmed him and brought him a happiness that he hadn't known for years.

* * * * * * * *

The weather in spring was as foul as it had been in the autumn. The rain had come on in gentle showers in late April, but by mid-May had become a constant curse. Weather forecasters offered little optimism for an improvement, whilst newspapers talked of global warming, climate change and incessant rain becoming a permanent feature.

About seven months after the funeral, Clarke and Ned were on the south coast for the weekend. It was the first time Ned had been in Brighton since Jake's death.

The sea slapped against the dunes of pebbles beside the coast road with a roar that threatened menace above the whip-cracking of the wind. Unexpected gusts tested the strength of umbrellas. Collars were pulled high as passers-by dashed from shelter to shelter, hopping over kerbs and hurdling puddles in a hurry to avoid a drenching. Clarke and Ned stood hunched against the gale, whilst the wind bullied empty Coke cans down the promenade towards Brighton Pier.

Jake wasn't far from their thoughts. They had made a point of searching out the Royal Pavilion Hotel and now stood staring up at its facade, scanning the wrought-iron balconies, trying to pick out Jake's room, imagining the scene the morning he was found – the sea of vodka bottles and Jake's bloated face as he lay comatose on the bed. As they gazed up at the hotel, the freezing wind spat sea spray into their faces, just enough to mask the gathering sadness in their eyes.

Clarke reminded Ned that they were pressed for time by tapping at his watch. He turned and set off in a jog back to the car. Halfway there he stopped and called back to Ned – still staring at the hotel – and waved for him to hurry up.

"Ned..."

"What?"

"What was the worst refereeing decision you can remember?" Clarke shouted through a cupped hand pressed to Ned's ear as they struggled through the rain.

"WHAT?"

"What was the worst refereeing decision you can remember?"

"God, I don't know... why?"

"I was just thinking– "

"What? In any sport?"

Ned knew that there was no way back now, trying to get the conversation finished so that they could get out of the rain.

"Any sport." Clarke answered quickly.

"Oh God, I don't know... Why?"

"Oh, I was just thinking about Webb Ellis."

"*Who?*"

"Webb Ellis... The guy at Rugby School who invented rugby."

"What?"

"The boy at Rugby School... who picked the ball up during a game of soccer and ran with it in his hands and invented rugby."

"What of it?" Ned asked, growing impatient.

"It was a deliberate act of foul play. Why didn't the referee send him off?"

"Jesus, I don't know, Charlie."

"He could at least have given a free kick for handball. But oh no... he just says something like: 'Well done, Webb Ellis... we'll call that game rugby. Congratulations, you've just invented a new sport for fat blokes... Oh, and I'll tell you what... we'll make the ball egg-shaped... Terrible decision. He should have sent him off... I'll never understand the English."

"Christ, Charlie. I worry about you sometimes."

When they got to the car, Clarke's mobile rang. He was surprised. His new mobile was almost as unreliable as his old one in the damp. He rarely got calls.

"Hello... can I help you?"

"Charlie. It's me."

"Who's that?"

It was a woman's voice.

"Have you forgotten me already, Charlie? I know it's been a while, but– "

"Jesus... It's you, isn't it?"

He trembled. It was Jane Etherington.

"I am so glad you called me."

"Well, I'm surprised to hear you say that after the last time... Charlie, look, I need to talk to you."

She sounded panicky. He thought it uncharacteristic.

"Yeah sure, of course... No problem. What about?"

"I can't tell you over the phone. We'll have to meet up in London sometime."

"No problem... Where are you right now?"

"At home."

"Same home?"

"Same home."

"Shall I come over tonight?"

"No. Actually, I'm going up to stay with my sister for a while."

"Where's that?"

"Oban."

"Jesus! When are you leaving?"

"Now."

"How long for?"

"A couple of months... maybe longer."

"What? God, Jane... What is it you want to tell me? Er... how were you going to tell me?"

"Look, I can't tell you over the phone."

"So why the hell are you phoning me?"

"Oh... I don't know... but I do have to see you."

"Well, can I come up to Oban?"

"What? Why would you want to do that?"

"To see you."

"Really?"

"Yeah... Why not? Oh for God's sake just tell me what it is."

"Would you really come up to Oban just to see me?"

"I'll walk on bloody tiptoe, if you tell me what the hell it is you want to– "

"I'm pregnant."

"What!"

"Pregnant."

"How pregnant?"

"Very."

"How pregnant is that?"

"Seven months."

"What? No! Who?"

"You."

"Me?"

"You."

"No."

"Yes."

"Jesus... that's amazing... I'm too old!"

"Obviously not."

"That's amazing!"

"So, do you still want to come to Oban?"

"Er... Yes... Of course."

"So, can I tell you something else?"

"What?"

"I'm probably not going to come back."

"From Oban?"

"Yeah."

"Oh."

"Come up. I'll show you round. Maybe you'll like it. Maybe you'll want to stay."

"Really?"

"Maybe... Call me on my mobile when you get back from whatever you're doing now and I'll give you the address blah, blah, blah."

"Sure."

"Bye sweetie," she said, and was gone.

Clarke looked round for Ned, who was clambering into the driver's seat and covering Clarke in a fine spray of rainwater. Clarke leant over and kissed him.

"Look, Charlie, I don't think that's a very goo– "

"That was Jane."

"Jane who?"

"Jane Etherington."

"Jane Etherington?"

"Yes."

"What did she want?"

"Me."

"Great," Ned said matter-of-factly, whilst switching on the ignition and over-revving the engine. He was anxious to get going, not wanting to be late for the game. Chelsea versus Brighton. A cup match. Neither of them wanted to miss the kick-off, keen to get a good spot on the terrace behind the goal in Goldstone Road.

If you liked that, try this...

The room in dull grey light seemed more of a cell than an office. The gentle ticking of a clock was the only reminder that the working day would end. The tired silhouettes of the subs on the late shift suggested time unwinding in slow motion.

Jenkins fought off the lethargy of a long day. He had a piece to finish for Thursday's paper. Dedication had already prolonged his captivity well beyond the twilight departure of the nine-to-fivers. He had smoked on through the evening and into the night, struggling to tease the appropriate words onto the screen before him.

There were few words to describe drug-trafficking in Northern Ireland that hadn't been used before. The mainstream politicians had nothing new to say. The RUC press office had supplied the same gloomy statistics. The paramilitaries issued their standard denials. Mantra.

The emergence of the drugs market was a story that needed to be told repeatedly, but was one which no one wanted to hear. Not now. In Belfast people were preoccupied with avoiding bombs and bullets. In Westminster, government was preoccupied with taming the unions.

By four in the morning, however, Jenkins had found an angle he reckoned he could flesh out and that his editor would print. His feature might keep the story alive a little longer. He hoped it would satisfy his sources and wouldn't get him shot. But for such a large man he was a small target.

An excerpt from 'The Island', Nick Cann's second novel available from October 1st 2005